The Clockwise Man

Collect all the exciting new Doctor Who *adventures:*

THE MONSTERS INSIDE
By Stephen Cole

WINNER TAKES ALL
By Jacqueline Rayner

The
Clockwise Man

BY JUSTIN RICHARDS

BOOKS

Published in 2005 by BBC Books, an imprint of Ebury Publishing
Ebury Publishing is a division of the Random House Group

The Random House Group Limited Reg. No. 954009
Addresses for companies within the Random House Group can be found at
www.randomhouse.co.uk

A CIP catalogue record for this book is available from the British Library

The Random House Group Limited makes every effort to ensure that the
papers used in our books are made from trees that have been legally sourced
from well-managed and credibly certified forests. Our paper procurement
policy can be found on www.randomhouse.co.uk

Commissioning Editors: Shirley Patton/Stuart Cooper
Creative Director: Justin Richards
Editor: Stephen Cole

Doctor Who is a BBC Wales production for BBC ONE
Executive Producers: Russell T Davies, Julie Gardner and Mal Young
Producer: Phil Collinson

Cover design by Henry Steadman © BBC 2005
Typeset in Albertina by Rocket Editorial, Aylesbury, Bucks
Printed and bound in Great Britain by
Cox & Wyman Ltd, Reading, Berkshire

For Julian and Christian – and everyone else now discovering or rediscovering the amazing worlds of Doctor Who

Peter Dickson learned the truth about black cats from his mother.

'If a black cat comes up to you,' she said to him, 'then that's lucky, that is. But if it only comes part-way, then turns back… If it has burning green eyes…' She sucked in her breath and shook her head. 'They say that your father saw a black cat that morning, on the way to his ship. I reckon it had green eyes. I reckon he should have come home that moment, like any sensible sailor. He'd still be here now if he'd paid attention to that black cat. They're fickle animals, cats. Don't trust them. They only ever think of themselves. If they bring you luck, good or bad, you can be sure it's for their own reasons.'

The black cat Dickson saw almost thirty years later was neither approaching nor turning tail. It watched him from across the street with glassy reflective eyes. It was impossible to tell what colour they really were – was that lucky or not? Dickson took a deep breath of smoggy London air. He neither knew nor cared. He wasn't superstitious, like his old mother – a Victorian woman in every sense, he thought. And anyway, you couldn't even tell what colour the cat itself was – it just looked black because it was dark. There was a smudge of pale colouring under its chin, a triangle of white in the darkness below the glint of the eyes. Then, in an instant, the cat was gone. As if the eyes had been switched off.

Dickson blew out a stream of smoke from his cigarette. A final drag before he went back into the house. The guests would be arriving soon, and he needed to ensure everything was ready. He flicked away the stub end of the cigarette and watched it glow briefly before fading and dying. Like the eyes of the cat. He coughed in the cold October air, and turned to go back inside.

Rose looked down at herself, wondering how daft she seemed. Did they really dress like this in the 1920s – thin cotton down to the calf? And in mint green? She had found a long, dark cloak with a hood, which she dumped across the TARDIS console.

The Doctor spared her a glance. He was tapping at some meter or other. Satisfied, he nodded and moved to the next control – which was covered by Rose's cloak. A brief frown, and the Doctor moved on. Rose watched his fiercely intense eyes reflecting the light of the console as he focused on the next control. She liked the way he stood so still and so confident – yet any second she knew he might break into a broad grin.

Seeming to realise he was being watched, he looked up at her again. 'What?'

'Are we nearly there yet?'

'You sound like a kid on an outing.'

'I am a kid on an outing. An outing back in time.' She couldn't help smiling at the prospect, and he grinned back.

'Yeah. Great, isn't it? It's 1924 out there. Or will be in a mo.' He tapped encouragingly on a control.

'And that's when this exhibition thing is?'

'The British Empire Exhibition, yeah. Got to get a bit of culture now and then.'

Rose laughed. 'Like a school trip. Tell me again – why do I want to see it?'

He blinked in feigned disbelief. 'Because your best mate's going.'

That made her grin. 'So why doesn't he have to dress up for it?'

He was shocked now, standing back from the console and gesturing at his own clothes. Leather jacket over a dark brown round-necked shirt, faded slacks and battered shoes. 'Excuse me,' he said, pointing. 'New shirt.'

Without waiting for her verdict on the shirt, he turned to the scanner. The picture was dark, too dark to see anything at first. Then the blackness softened into shapes as the contrast and brightness adjusted.

'We could try infrared,' the Doctor muttered. 'But I don't think there's much heat out there.'

Rose could dimly make out some of the shapes now – ironwork and wooden planks; an old bedstead and a pile of buckets. 'It's cold and we're in a scrapyard.'

The Doctor shrugged. 'I like scrapyards. Never know what

you might find.' He checked another reading. 'You'll need that cloak,' he said, as if noticing it for the first time. The doors opened, and a faint trace of mist wafted in from the yard.

'Reckon we'll meet anyone famous?' Rose wondered.

'In October 1924?'

'They did have famous people then, right?'

His voice floated back from the misty outside. 'No television, but yeah they did.'

Rose hurried after him, into the excitement of the unknown.

At first he had thought it was the cat, fighting with something. Making an awful howling noise. But there was something rhythmic and mechanical about the sound that split the night air. It was not a sound made by an animal. A grating, rasping sound like some great engine grinding into life, then dying. Over and over. It came from everywhere and nowhere – whichever way he turned, the sound was already echoing back to him.

A flash of light from behind the gate into Gibson's Yard. For a moment, Dickson saw the glow over the wooden gate, and the light shining between the planks. Then it was gone, and the sound had ended in a satisfied thump.

'Who's there?' Dickson called out. But his voice was brittle and scratchy. He could barely hear himself. He glanced back at the house, considered going back inside. But he was curious about the sound and the light. Dickson made his way down the steps from the side door and headed for the gate to Gibson's Yard.

He crossed the street, not noticing the black cat that slunk away down the street, flicking its tail as it went. He made his careful way towards the heavy wooden gate, oblivious to how the shadows behind him seemed to deepen and grow. Was that the sound of a door opening? Were there voices?

The shadow behind him quickened pace, its quarry now within its grasp. Its inhuman fingers stretched out, trembling rhythmically, clicking towards the back of Dickson's neck.

In the distance Dickson could hear Big Ben chiming the half-hour. He hesitated, the hairs on the back of his neck prickling as if in a faint breeze. Suddenly his every sense was straining. He could see a pale glow of light from behind the gate. Feel the cool night air on his skin. Smell the damp of the Thames wafted on the breeze. For some reason he could taste the rusty iron of blood in his mouth, as if he had bitten his tongue.

And to his amazement, as the chiming stopped, he was sure he could hear the ticking of Big Ben, marking off the remaining seconds of his life.

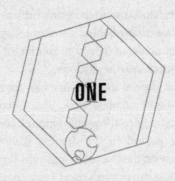

ONE

The air was cold with a smell of damp and smog. Rose pulled the cloak tight about her and ran over to the Doctor. He was inspecting a large wooden gate, his sonic screwdriver poised over the lock, glowing busily.

'Breaking and exiting?' Rose suggested. Her breath misted the air as she spoke.

The Doctor did not look up. 'Someone's in trouble – can't you hear?'

Now that he said it, she could. In among the noise of the city – the clatter of distant wheels on cobbles, the far-off sounds of people shouting and calling, the melancholy hoot of a boat on the Thames... Over and above that she could hear the muffled cries of someone in pain, or fear.

The sonic screwdriver hummed, and the lock clicked open. The Doctor was already kicking at the heavy gate, sending it flying back as he hurtled through.

Fifty feet away, startled in the pale glow of a street lamp, a man was fighting for his life. His assailant was forcing him backwards, its hands round the man's neck as it bore down on him. A dark shape behind the struggling figures – all silhouette and no detail. The vague notion of a third figure disappearing back into the shadows.

The Doctor crashed shoulder-first into the attacker. Hold broken, the figure stepped back. The Doctor collapsed, clutching his shoulder, then pulled himself back to his feet. The attacker paused in the deepest shadows, deciding whether to take on the Doctor as well as its first victim.

'Doctor!' Rose ran towards them. Her appearance seemed to decide it, and the dark figure turned and marched stiffly away. Watching the figure, trying to make out some feature in the dim light, Rose caught her foot on the kerb and went sprawling. She put out her hands to save herself, feeling the rough surface of the pavement cutting into them, rubbing away the skin. She came to rest in an undignified heap close to the man who had been attacked.

He was lying gasping on the ground, rubbing at his throat. He was wearing white gloves, but now they were stained and dirty. The Doctor leaned over and loosened the man's collar. 'Has he gone?' he asked without looking at Rose.

'Yeah. I scared him off.' She got to her feet, shrugging the cloak back over her shoulders and examining her hands – grazed, sore and covered in mud. Typical.

'I'm glad someone did.' The Doctor straightened up and rubbed his shoulder again. 'It was like running into a brick wall.'

Rose stooped to help the man on the ground. He was breathing more easily now and struggling to sit up. 'Thank you,' he croaked. 'I'm obliged.'

'You're alive,' the Doctor said. He put his hand under the man's elbow and helped him up.

'Who was that?' Rose asked. 'Why did he attack you?'

'I have no idea, miss. I heard a noise, saw lights. I came to see what it was and…' He shrugged, still rubbing at his neck.

'Here, let's see.' The Doctor led him a few steps down the pavement so they were directly under the street light. He gestured for the man to raise his head. 'It's all right, I'm a doctor.'

'Just not a medical one,' Rose pointed out, earning a glare. 'So, is he OK?'

'Dickson, miss.'

'Mr Dickson will be fine,' the Doctor said. 'Lucky we got here when we did, though. Where do you live?'

'I am in service, sir, at the house over there.' Dickson pointed to a large town house further down the street. Rose could see that the side door was open and light was spilling out down the steps.

'Then let's get you back there.' The Doctor stepped away, looking Dickson up and down. He frowned and reached for the man's hand, lifted it gently in his own to examine it in the light. Apparently satisfied, he smiled, let the hand go, gestured for Dickson to lead the way. He took Dickson's arm to help him.

'What is it?' Rose asked quietly.

'You keep your gloves clean, Mr Dickson?'

'Of course, sir.' He still sounded hoarse, his voice scraping in his throat. 'Why?'

'Just they're a bit grubby now, after your little adventure. Another mystery.'

'To go with "who?" and "why?",' Rose said.

'To go with the fact that the marks on Mr Dickson's neck look like they were made by a metal implement, not fingers,' the Doctor said. 'And that his gloves are stained with oil.'

From the darkest part of the shadowy evening, two figures watched the Doctor and Rose help Dickson back to the house. One of them gave a sigh of disappointment.

The other had no breath with which to sigh.

After the third attempt, Sir George Harding gave up. 'Give me a hand with this, would you, Anna?'

His wife was smiling back at him in the mirror, amused by his clumsiness. 'You are all fingers and thumbs,' she said softly, as she reached round to sort out the mess he had made of his bow tie. Her accent made her voice sound even softer. He held still while she tied a perfect bow. Then she turned him slowly round and stepped back to inspect her work. She nodded. 'Yes, my dear. You will do.'

'Good. They'll be here soon. Surprised Oblonsky hasn't arrived already, actually. He's always early, drat him. Must be the military training.'

The doorbell sounded insistently from downstairs.

'You see? That'll be him now. Playing Wagner on the bell.'

'Tchaikovsky, more likely,' Anna said. 'Dickson will look after him until we are ready.'

Sir George nodded. 'Yes, good man, Dickson.' He reached

for his jacket. 'Where's Freddie?'

'In bed. And I don't want you going in and disturbing him. Dilys has only just got him settled, and you know you only excite the child.'

'Me?' Sir George was scandalised. 'Never!'

'We have to keep him calm. Calm and safe.' She turned away, but he could still see her sad face reflected in the mirror. 'You know that.'

'Of course I do.' He put his hand on her trembling shoulder. 'The boy will be all right. We mustn't fuss too much, you know.'

She reached up, put her hand over his without turning, nodded without smiling. If she was about to reply, she was interrupted by the urgent knock at the door, then the frightened call: 'Sir, madam! Can you come, please? Only it's Mr Dickson, he's been hurt. There's a lady and gentleman…'

The Doctor insisted on taking Dickson to the front door and ringing the bell. No point, he said, in dragging him through the servants' quarters. 'If in doubt, go to the top.'

The woman who eventually opened the door looked about sixteen, little more than a kid. She was wearing an apron, wiping her hands on it. 'Mr Dickson, sir!' she exclaimed.

'He'll be fine,' the Doctor assured her, helping Dickson into the extensive hallway.

'Could you inform Sir George,' Dickson croaked.

The girl nodded silently, looking pale as she saw the red marks on Dickson's neck. She turned and ran up the stairs, holding up apron and skirts. The stairs turned halfway up, and Rose could see the girl on the galleried landing, flickering behind the balusters as she ran.

'Let's put you in here,' the Doctor said, leading Dickson through to a large room.

Dickson tried to pull away. 'But that's the drawing room, sir.'

'I don't mind.'

'And I don't draw,' Rose told him.

It was a large, square room with a high ceiling. Dark oil portraits leaned in from several walls, the severe expressions of the subjects making the place seem even darker. Three long sofas dominated the centre of the room, arranged in front of a huge fireplace. The logs on the fire crackled and smoked.

The Doctor helped Dickson to the nearest sofa and sat him down. 'Let's get a proper look at those bruises.'

'I'll be fine, sir,' Dickson protested. 'I should get to work. We are expecting guests.'

'Guests can wait,' Rose told him.

'Indeed they can, young lady.'

She turned quickly, surprised by the voice from behind her. A man was standing in the doorway. He looked to be in his fifties, hair grey and thinning, slicked back over his pale scalp. He was wearing a suit that was just too small. Rose doubted the jacket would do up. His whole appearance was slightly down at heel and dishevelled except for his perfect bow tie. But his face was round and kindly. His eyes sparkled with interest and friendliness, though this changed to concern as he looked past Rose and saw Dickson slumped on the sofa. He hurried across, mumbling an 'excuse me', as he passed Rose. She followed him to the sofa and stood behind it as he leaned over Dickson.

'I'll be fine, sir,' Dickson croaked. The doorbell rang, and he struggled to get up.

But the newcomer gently pushed him back into the sofa. 'Nonsense, man. You sit there for a bit. Let us sort you out. Dilys can answer the door.' He raised his voice and shouted across towards the open door: 'Put them in the library, Dilys.'

'This gentleman and the lady helped me, sir,' Dickson said. 'I was... attacked.' He seemed to surprise himself with the word, as if it had not occurred to him until now what had really happened.

'Who by?' the man – Sir George, Rose assumed – demanded.

Dickson was shaking his head. 'Not sure, sir. Didn't see. But they were asking questions, or someone was. Someone else who was there, I think.'

'Questions?'

'About tonight. About the guests.'

Sir George reached out to the arm of the sofa and lowered himself carefully down beside his manservant. 'They have found us,' he said, so quietly that Rose could only just hear him. She looked at the Doctor, and saw that he had heard too.

'These people rescued me,' Dickson said.

Sir George was staring off into space. But Dickson's words seemed to bring him back to reality. 'I am indebted, sir, madam.' He nodded. 'Very much indebted. I thank you.' He stood up, squared his shoulders and solemnly offered the

Doctor his hand. 'Sir George Harding. I apologise if you have been inconvenienced.'

'No problem,' the Doctor assured him, shaking his hand.

Rose nipped round the sofa and took Sir George's hand when the Doctor was done with it. 'Rose Tyler,' she said, smiling at him. 'And this is the Doctor.'

'A medical man?'

'Not really,' the Doctor admitted. 'But I know a thing or two.' He sucked in his cheeks. 'You were expecting this?'

'No,' Sir George said at once. 'Well, no more than anyone else. There have been several… incidents locally in the last few months. Those of us with any small wealth or possessions always fear the worst.'

The Doctor nodded, as if he completely understood. 'But some more than others, perhaps.'

'They're expecting guests,' Rose reminded him. 'We should leave them to it. If Mr Dickson's OK.'

'I'll be fine, miss, thank you,' he croaked.

'We have a fairly full table,' Sir George said, 'but the least I can do under the circumstances is offer you some dinner.' He seemed genuinely eager for them to stay. 'Shouldn't be too much of a squeeze and cook always provides far more than we need.'

'Thank you, Sir George,' the Doctor said. 'But I'm sure we'd be in the way.'

'As you wish.'

'Another time, p'raps,' Rose said.

'Well, let me offer you a drink at least.'

'In the library?' the Doctor asked.

'Does it matter where?'

'Of course. I love books.'

Rose cleared her throat. 'I'd love a drink too,' she said. 'But, maybe I can wash my hands?'

The Doctor was at once concerned as she showed them her palms – muddy and scraped, lines of dried blood tracing out the scratches from where she had fallen. 'Is it still bleeding? I can cauterise the wounds with my sonic –'

'No, thanks,' she said quickly. 'I'll be fine. I just need to wash the mud off and clean up a bit. That's all.'

Sir George took a step backwards, looking pale. 'I'm sorry,' he said. 'The sight of blood. I know it's not much, but just the thought of it…' He sighed and forced a smile. 'Forgive me. So long as there's no real harm done.'

'I'll show Miss Tyler to the guest bathroom,' Dickson said. Sir George looked dubious, but Dickson got to his feet, determined. 'It is the least that I can do, sir.'

'Very well.' Sir George smiled at Rose. 'Join us as soon as you wish.' His smile broadened as he looked past Rose towards the door. 'Ah, my dear. Let me introduce Miss Tyler and Doctor umm…' He glanced at the Doctor, but got no help. 'And the Doctor,' he finished.

A woman had come in. She looked much younger than Sir George, though Rose guessed she was older than she seemed. She was tall and slim, elegantly dressed ready for dinner. Her hair was fixed up elaborately, grey streaked with the last vestiges of blonde.

'My wife, Anna,' Sir George said, and his affection for her was evident in his voice.

'Everyone is here, George, if you are ready to join us,' Anna said. Rose could see the lines of worry etched round the woman's eyes, though she was smiling now. 'Or almost everyone.'

'Knew Oblonsky would be here on time,' Sir George mumbled. 'So who are we waiting for? That Repple fellow and his companion?'

'No, Mr Repple is here. We're just waiting for the Painted Lady.'

Everything in the bathroom was big and chunky. Even the taps on the large square washbasin were large silver affairs with ears sticking out of the top. But the water ran hot, and once the stinging from the soap – a big, chunky bar of soap – had subsided, the water was soothing. Rose spent several minutes with her hands plunged into the warm water, watching her face blur and fade as the mirror over the basin misted to grey.

Dickson had taken her cloak, and she was feeling less worried about her pale green dress now that she had seen what Sir George's wife, Anna, was wearing. And no one had remarked on her clothes, one way or another. So maybe the Doctor was right and they would simply blend in, despite his own unorthodox approach.

Leaving the bathroom, Rose started down the corridor back towards the stairs. At least, she realised as she made her way past several closed doors, she thought this was the way back to the stairs. Surely the bathroom had been on their left. Or had it? She paused, trying to remember. There was a bend in the corridor ahead of her. Did she recall that? Maybe the stairs were just the other side of the turn.

But they were not. Back the other way then, she decided. She felt a pang of unreasonable guilt as one of the doors close to her swung open. A face peered out from the darkness beyond. A boy of about ten, with fair hair. His eyes widened as he caught sight of Rose, and the door began to swing shut again.

'No, wait,' she called. 'I'm lost, can you help?'

The door opened again, more cautiously this time. She could see the shape of the boy's head against the darkness inside. 'Who are you? Are you here for the party?'

'I don't know about that. I'm looking for the library. I'm supposed to see my friend there for a drink before we leave.'

The boy's head poked out into the light and he inspected her. 'I'm supposed to be asleep,' he said.

'Well, just tell me the way back to the stairs, then. I'll find my way from there.' She took a step towards him, careful not to startle the boy. 'I'm Rose, nice to meet you.'

The boy sniffed, and shuffled out into the corridor. 'Freddie,' he said.

In the light she could see he was very pale. His eyes were the darkest thing about him – an almost deathly white face, fair hair that could do with a comb, and he was wearing pale blue striped pyjamas. The shape of his face was so like Anna's that it was obvious whose child he was. Rose might have laughed at the shuffling figure, but for the crutch. He had it crooked under his left arm and leaned on it as he shuffled forwards. She tried not to look at it, not to make him aware that she had noticed.

'I can walk without it,' he said. 'But it's harder, when I'm tired.'

Good one, Rose, she thought. 'Shouldn't you be in bed?' she said. 'Your mum and dad have guests.'

'Mother and stepfather,' he corrected her. 'Like I said, they think I'm asleep, but I want to see who's coming. Sometimes they let me stay up.'

'But not tonight.'

He shook his head. 'They're in the library?'

Rose nodded.

'I'll show you the secret way,' Freddie said. He set off down the corridor, surprisingly quickly, hardly leaning on the crutch at all. 'Come on.'

Rose was soon lost as Freddie led her down another passageway. This one was more narrow, the walls panelled with dark wood. He paused before several steps up to a small door.

'Shhh.' Freddie put his finger to his lips. 'You'll have to be quiet. We can whisper, but we mustn't let them hear, or…'

'Or your stepfather will give you a good thrashing?' Rose wondered. He had not seemed the type, but she could imagine Freddie did not want to anger Sir George.

The boy's answer surprised her. 'He wouldn't dare,' he said quietly. Then he opened the door and stepped through.

Rose followed and found herself on a narrow wooden gallery. Freddie was sitting on the floor, his crutch beside him. He had produced a small notebook and a stub of pencil and was scribbling away. He put his finger to his lips again as he caught sight of Rose, and motioned for her to sit down beside him on the bare wooden floor. Rose crouched down. She could already hear the sounds of voices from the room below, and now she saw that the gallery was high up above the library.

Further along there were wooden shelves, packed with dusty books. Steep steps spiralled down into the main room. The library itself was as big as the drawing room, and every wall was covered with bookshelves. She only realised where the door was when a section of shelving swung open to allow Dickson to enter. He seemed to have recovered from his ordeal and was wearing clean white gloves. He carried a round silver tray with glasses on. Rose watched him walk stiffly across to where the Doctor and Sir George were standing with several other people.

'Is that your friend?' Freddie whispered, pointing through the balusters.

'The Doctor, yeah.' She leaned forward to see what he was writing.

But Freddie snapped the notebook shut. 'Private,' he hissed.

'Sorry. Who are the others?'

Freddie eased himself further forward so he could see more easily. Rose wondered if the people below would notice them, but the gallery was unlit and it was unlikely anyone would look up so high.

'You know Mother and Father,' Freddie whispered, pointing them out.

Rose nodded. 'Stepfather, you said.'

'My real father died when I was two. Before we came here.'

'I'm sorry,' Rose murmured, but the boy seemed not to hear.

Freddie pointed to a large man, broad-shouldered and round-faced. He had a large bushy moustache that was as black as his hair, and he was wearing a smart, white military uniform. 'That's Colonel Oblonsky. He comes here a lot to see Father, and they talk in the study.' Freddie stifled a giggle. 'He salutes me and calls me sir.'

Rose smiled with him. The colonel looked so serious it was hard to imagine him playing with the child. 'And those two?' She pointed to a frail-looking couple who were sitting on upright chairs at the reading table, talking to Freddie's mother. They both looked in their seventies – a thin-faced man who was completely bald, his scalp crinkled and blotchy, and a woman who was painfully thin with hair as white as cotton wool and a jutting nose and chin. The woman reminded Rose of the wicked witch in Disney's *Snow White*, though her expression was kindly.

'They're cousins of Mother, or something. But I call them Uncle Alex and Aunt Nadia. They're very kind.'

This left only one other person – a man who had been taking a drink from Dickson's tray. He went over to join Colonel Oblonsky, who greeted him warmly.

'Lord Chitterington,' Freddie said. 'He works in the government. The British government,' he added, as if there might be any confusion. 'Father tells him off if he tries to play with me because he's too rough and I mustn't get hurt.'

That seemed to be everyone. Colonel Oblonsky and Lord Chitterington were standing almost below the gallery now, and Rose leaned forward slightly in an attempt to hear what they were saying. They certainly seemed very earnest. But she could make out only a few words and phrases from the louder Oblonsky.

'Did you talk with Reilly?' he was asking. 'Is he with us?'

Lord Chitterington replied in a quiet voice that Rose could not hear, and Oblonsky muttered something back.

But Rose was no longer listening. She had all but dismissed the other guests from her mind. Further under the gallery stood two more people. She caught barely a glimpse of them, except that Sir George had now excused himself from the Doctor and joined the two men. Their voices were clear, floating up through the gallery to where Rose and Freddie were sitting.

'I trust you are not bored already with our company,' Sir George was saying.

'Who are they?' Rose mouthed to Freddie, suddenly worried that the men below might hear her. Freddie shrugged and shook his head. Rose strained to hear, listening so intently she could just make out a clock ticking somewhere under the gallery.

'Forgive me, Sir George,' one of the men replied. His voice was clear and without a noticeable accent. Upper class without being posh. English without a region. 'Major Aske and myself have had a long day. And you will appreciate that until we hear what you have to say I am not inclined to give away too much about my own plans and ambitions.'

'Of course, sir. I quite understand.'

The second man – Major Aske – said, 'But Repple is keen to offer what help he can to your noble cause. We can see, as you can, the similarity between your own plight and ours.'

'Or rather, the boy's plight,' the first man – Repple – added. Rose saw Freddie frown at the words. Perhaps they were talking about a different boy.

'You are very kind. And it is good of you to accept my invitation,' Sir George said. 'Forgive me, sir, but I am not sure quite how you prefer to be addressed.'

'Until I can use my proper title without fear or competition, I use none. Please address me simply as Repple.'

The general sound of people talking seemed to increase, perhaps as the guests drank and felt more at ease. It made it difficult to catch anything other than the odd word here and there. Beside Rose, Freddie was yawning.

'I think it's time to go,' Rose whispered. 'You need to get back to bed.'

The boy looked for a moment as if he was about to protest. But then he yawned again, and that seemed to convince him and he nodded. Rose helped him to his feet and they crept quietly from the gallery and back down the narrow passage beyond.

On the way back to his room, Freddie hardly seemed to use his crutch. 'Is your leg feeling better?' Rose asked.

'It just gets tired,' he said, as if it was nothing. 'Mum likes me to use the crutch at home so I won't fall and hurt myself. I don't use it in public. That would look like weakness.'

They were back at his room now. Freddie opened the door, and paused long enough to give Rose quick directions to the main stairs. He turned to go inside, then changed his mind and turned back.

'Thank you, Rose,' he said.

She laughed. 'For what? You're helping me, remember?'

He nodded, suddenly solemn. 'It was fun though, seeing the grown-ups.' He yawned again, then went inside the room. 'Goodbye.' The door closed quietly behind him.

'They seemed like nice enough people,' Rose said. She had found her way to the library and the Doctor had introduced her to everyone Freddie had already pointed out. Rose was impressed he could remember all their names.

Uncle Alex and Aunt Nadia, the Doctor introduced as Count Alexander and Countess Nadia Koznyshev. They spoke with heavy accents which Rose guessed were Russian. The two men under the gallery – Repple and Major Aske – were both tall and slim, and looked like soldiers, though they were dressed smartly in dark suits. Aske seemed younger, perhaps in his late twenties, with light brown hair and a smattering of freckles across his lean face. He stood very straight, with one hand permanently in his jacket pocket. Repple had a darker complexion – his hair was black as night, and his features were handsome and symmetrical. Rose found herself looking at him for longer than she should, to the Doctor's undisguised amusement.

But there was something about the atmosphere in the library as the people waited for the last guest, something strained and slightly awkward. Rose had played the goose-berry often enough to know that it was the presence of herself and the Doctor that was the stifling factor. She got the impression that everyone else was waiting for them to leave so they could get on with whatever it was they really wanted to be doing.

The mist was thickening as they made their way back down the street towards the yard where the TARDIS had landed. The gates were closed again, and to the Doctor's evident annoyance they were once more locked. He sighed and produced his sonic screwdriver from his coat pocket.

'I don't know what they're up to,' he confessed, setting to work once more on the lock. 'But they're certainly hiding something.'

'Something that got poor Dickson attacked?'

The Doctor made a noncommittal sound and the lock clicked open. 'Sir George seemed to think so, only he wouldn't admit it.' He pushed open the gate and stared into the darkness of the yard.

'Not that it matters to us, I guess,' Rose said. 'What do we do, sit around till morning or just move on?'

'It might matter a lot,' the Doctor said. He made no attempt to enter the yard, just stood there in the gateway, staring in. He gave the gate a shove so that it swung open, allowing Rose to see into the yard as well.

The empty yard.

'Because,' the Doctor continued in the same matter-of-fact tone as the first rain began to fall, 'it might be whoever attacked Dickson that took the TARDIS.'

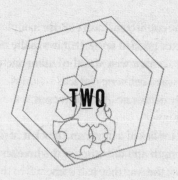

TWO

They spent what seemed like for ever pacing the damp streets. The air was so damp it was hard to tell if it was mist or drizzle. At first, Rose thought the Doctor had a definite plan, that he had some idea where to look for the TARDIS. But after following him down yet another street she realised he had no better idea than she did.

'Think, think, think,' he hissed to himself as they stood on a nondescript street corner beside a postbox, its red the only colour in the grey-dark world.

'Maybe someone just took a fancy to it,' Rose suggested.

'Not likely. Big coincidence.'

'So someone saw us arrive. Or knows what the TARDIS is.'

'Maybe.' He wiggled his fingers encouragingly. 'More ideas, more clues.'

'Someone attacked Dickson, right? We saved him. Maybe that naffed them off.'

'Could be. More?'

'Got to be connected, hasn't it?' she said.

The Doctor nodded several times rapidly. 'Seems likely.'

'And Sir George was afraid of someone or something. Thought it was a deliberate attack.'

'Certainly deliberate. And motivated.'

'So what now?'

The Doctor licked a finger and stuck it in the air as if testing the strength and direction of the breeze. 'That way.' He pointed back the way they had come.

'Sure?'

'Positive.' He set off at a confident jog.

'To the TARDIS?' It seemed to Rose that it was as good as found.

But his response dampened her spirits as much as the increasing rain. 'Nah. Back to Sir George. That's the only connection – the only clue we've got.'

'Hope you remember the way.'

The light drizzle quickly turned to heavy rain, and they had to dance round the growing puddles. They arrived back at the house just as a large black car was drawing up. The driver was a blank silhouette against the light from the house. There was the outline of a woman sitting in the back.

Dickson appeared as if by intuition, complete with unfurled umbrella which he put up as he hurried down the steps. His eyes widened slightly in well-disguised surprise as he saw the Doctor and Rose.

'We decided to take up the offer of dinner after all,' the Doctor told him.

'If it's still open,' Rose added.

'I am sure it is, sir. Please, do go in. I shall be with you in a moment.' Dickson returned his professional attention to holding the umbrella over the woman from the back of the car as she stepped out on to the pavement.

'He might have offered us the umbrella,' Rose complained, shaking the water out of her hair and brushing it off her cloak.

'And let the paint run?'

'What do you mean?'

For an answer, the Doctor nodded at the woman now stepping into the hallway behind them. Dickson stood in the doorway behind her, putting down the umbrella.

But Rose's attention was fixed on the woman. On her face. She looked as if she had stepped out of a masked ball. Her dress was pale, shimmering silk, blowing round her in the breeze from the open door. Her flame-red hair was allowed to cascade down to her bare shoulders. But her face was covered with a thin mask in the shape of a butterfly, so that only her mouth was visible. The mask was painted in bright colours – yellow, red, blue and green – and scattered with sequins. A delicate blue feather framed each side of it, contrasting with the red of her hair. Startlingly blue eyes looked out unblinkingly through almond-shaped holes.

'How do you do?' she said, her voice soft and cloying as honey. 'I don't believe we have met.' She held out a hand to the Doctor, and Rose saw that her white glove reached up to her elbow. From the way she angled the back of her hand towards him, it was obvious the Doctor was expected to kiss it. But instead he took it gently and gave it a polite shake.

'I'm the Doctor,' he said. 'And this is my friend Rose.'

The woman nodded, any disappointment hidden behind the mask. 'Melissa Heart,' she said. She nodded slightly at Rose, an acknowledgement, no more. 'I assume that you, like me, are here for the conspiracy.'

Despite the presence of Melissa Heart – apologising profusely for having missed dinner – it was a reduced company that sat in the dining room. Dinner had been cleared away, and they sat drinking pale wine from small multi-faceted glasses. The Doctor, Rose and Melissa sat in the spare chairs – recently vacated at the departure of the Koznyshevs and Lord Chitterington.

At least there were fewer names to remember, Rose thought, even if there was nothing left to eat except a disappointly small slice of apple pie.

The Doctor had apologised to Sir George and accepted the renewed offer of dinner. Or at least dessert. He had explained that they had been 'let down' and lost their lodgings. Sir George immediately offered to let them stay at the house, but his wife gently pointed out that they already had guests and it might be rather crowded.

'No problem,' the Doctor said. 'We'll find a hotel or something.'

'There are rooms at the Imperial Club,' Repple announced. 'I'm sure we can vouch for you there, at least for a day or two until you find alternative accommodation.'

'I'm so glad that's settled,' Melissa Heart said, clapping her hands together in apparent delight. 'I have only just moved into my own house – Anthony Hubbard's old house, by the river, perhaps you know it? But, as I say, I have barely unpacked, so I'm afraid accommodation would be difficult.'

The Doctor fielded the various obvious and polite questions that accompanied the arrival of the apple pie. They were in London for a few days to see the British Empire Exhibition. Yes, they were looking forward to it. Yes, they knew the city but had been out of town for a while. Travelling. The expressionless face of Melissa Heart – the Painted Lady, as Rose remembered someone had called her – watched the Doctor intently as he spoke, seeming to absorb his every word.

'So,' the Doctor said as he poked his spoon at his pie, 'what's this conspiracy all about?'

The sudden silence was broken by the sound of someone's involuntary gasp.

'Don't want to talk about it?' The Doctor shrugged and nodded sympathetically. He stood up, took off his leather jacket, and hung it over the back of the chair. Then he sat down again. 'Tell you what, then – why don't I guess?'

Rose looked round the table to see what reaction this provoked. Sir George was leaning back in his chair, if anything seeming slightly amused. His wife, by contrast, looked nervous and unsettled. Colonel Oblonsky had gone red and his lips quivered in anger. Aske, Repple and the Painted Lady were all equally impassive and unreadable.

The Doctor sniffed. 'Or we can finish our pud and leave you to get on with it. Thanks for the nosh. I don't want to impose or intrude.'

'How intriguing.' It was Melissa Heart who spoke. 'As a newcomer to this little group, I would be interested myself to hear the details. Interested also to see if what the Doctor has gleaned is anything approaching the truth.'

'And how do we know he is not a Bolshevik agent?' Oblonsky roared, his anger finally getting the better of him. 'I say we throw him into the street.' He leaned heavily forwards, scattering cutlery. 'Once we have determined how much he knows and who he is working for.'

'I'm no one's agent,' the Doctor said quietly.

'Gentlemen, please.' Sir George stood up, tossing his napkin down on his side plate. But Oblonsky paid no attention, continuing to stare malevolently at the Doctor and Rose.

It was Major Aske who calmed the situation. He cleared his throat, and said quietly, 'I doubt a Bolshevik agent, or any sort of agent, would be so bold as to invite himself to dinner and offer to explain your plans, Colonel. Repple and I are constantly alert to the possibility of spies, infiltrators, agents and assassins.'

Repple held up his hand as Aske finished speaking. 'The Doctor is obviously none of these. He and his companion may be able to help. Let us keep an open mind.'

Oblonsky leaned back, folding his arms, still angry. 'I am yet to be convinced.'

'Well that's a start,' the Doctor said happily. He raised his glass in a mock toast, then sipped at the wine. 'Mmm, 1917,' he declared.

'Not even close,' Sir George said. 'It's a 1921 claret.'

'I didn't mean the wine,' the Doctor said sternly. 'Though

if I did I might tell you the grapes came from a small vineyard just outside Briançon. No,' he went on quickly enough for Rose to guess he had made this up, 'I mean the Russian Revolution.'

'It's not hard to guess,' Rose said, seeing their surprised faces. Not that she had actually guessed until now. Not that she had a clue really what he was on about. 'There are a lot of Russians here. The colonel, the Koznyshevs earlier.'

'And Lady Anna,' the Doctor added.

Anna nodded, her raised eyebrows the only hint of her surprise. 'I left in October 1917. With my husband and my young son.'

'Your first husband,' Rose said, and was pleased to see the Doctor raise an eyebrow as Anna nodded.

'I had met Sir George when he was at the British Embassy in Moscow. He was the only person I knew well enough to ask for help when I got to London.' She reached across the table and took his hand.

'So,' Rose said, keen to make the most of her success so far, 'we have some dispossessed Russians, and Repple here is a man who has lost his title and wants it back. You all want to kick out Lenin and co. and reclaim your lost lands, is that it?' She grinned, pleased with herself.

The Painted Lady clapped her hands together in apparent admiration.

'No,' Colonel Oblonsky said.

'Oh.'

'She's close though,' the Doctor said. He grinned at her. 'Not bad.'

'Oh, cheers,' Rose muttered.

'She is right about me,' Repple said. He got to his feet and looked round. Aske sighed and turned away. But Repple ignored him. 'I shall not rest until I have reclaimed my birthright. No, not in Russia. Until the coup that took power from me, until I was branded a criminal and sent into exile, I was the Elector – the king if you will – of Dastaria. When I return, the people will rise up and drive out the oppressors who have laid waste our homeland.'

'Sir,' Aske said quietly, 'we shall triumph. But we must take it gently and slowly. Tread carefully. Capitalise on what support and allies we have. Not draw unwanted attention.'

'We must help our friends too,' Repple said. 'I am sorry that we can do little save lend our support and our name to your enterprise, my friends. But Dastaria shares a border with Russia. Your cause is a noble one. What help we can offer, we shall – even from exile.'

'I fear it will be little enough,' Aske said quietly.

'It would seem,' Oblonsky said, 'that you have a way of eliciting information, Doctor. Perhaps you are not an agent of Lenin or Trotsky and their lackeys. But now you know it all.'

The Doctor nodded. 'Almost all. For any chance of success so long after the revolution, you must have a trump card. Something you can use to rally support. Enthuse the people.'

'Go on,' Sir George prompted.

'I think you intend to return to Russia with the heir to the throne.' He grinned suddenly. 'Am I right, or am I right?' The silence was confirmation enough. All eyes were now on the Doctor.

Except for Rose's. She looked round at the other diners, and to her surprise she saw that while Melissa Heart's mask was facing the Doctor, her eyes were angled towards Repple.

'Now,' the Doctor went on, 'the colonel here could be the rightful Tsar of all the Russias. But he's more of a military man. Loyal soldier, yes? Succession doesn't include women for all sorts of ill-informed medieval reasons. So, I suggest the Tsar is… Count Koznyshev, though he didn't fancy the pie.' He sat back like a conjuror awaiting applause. There was only silence. 'In the ballroom?' he added hopefully. 'With the Fabergé egg?'

But Rose could see it now. An odd snatch of conversation, a strange comment, rose in her mind: 'He wouldn't dare.' She must have gasped out loud, because everyone had now turned towards her. 'It's Freddie, isn't it?' she said. 'Freddie is the rightful Tsar of Russia.'

The rest of the story – details and loose ends – came out as they finished the meal. Anna – Anastasia – was a cousin of Tsar Nicholas II and also related to Queen Victoria. Her first husband had been a cousin of the late Tsarina. With the Tsar and his immediate family dead, together with countless other relatives, the ten-year-old Frederick was next in the line of succession.

Colonel Oblonsky had been head of the Tsar's personal guard, and he seemed to blame himself for the success of the revolution. The Koznyshevs were loyal supporters of the Tsar. Lord Chitterington had been there to offer the clandestine support of the British government – support which he stressed would not extend to military intervention, but which might just run to financial help and diplomatic introductions.

Repple again made it clear that he could offer little more than supportive words until he was restored to his own throne. Maybe he was hoping to return to Dastaria with the help and intervention of a restored Tsar. Even without knowing how history was destined to turn out, it seemed to Rose that the 'conspirators' could do little more than talk and plan.

'Why are you here?' Rose asked Melissa Heart after the meal, as they headed towards the drawing room to continue their discussions.

'Oh, my dear,' she said, 'it will be such fun. And I have got to know so very many people since I came to London.'

But fun or not, Melissa Heart declined to join the others in the drawing room. She made her apologies, and left them in the hallway. 'I can see myself out,' she assured Dickson, who was carrying through a tantalus containing two decanters of port.

Rose lingered a moment in the hallway before following the others. Melissa Heart watched her from behind her mask, as if waiting for Rose to leave before she did. The effect was unsettling. Rose turned to follow the Doctor into the drawing room.

As she did so, she caught sight of something on the stairs – the faintest of movements from behind the balusters that ran along the landing. She paused, peering into the gloomy distance. A hand appeared, just for a moment, above the rail. It waved. Rose glanced at Melissa Heart to make sure she wasn't watching, then she waved quickly back.

'Goodnight, Freddie,' Rose murmured as she turned to go.

With Melissa gone, and Anna retired to bed, there was only Sir George, Colonel Oblonsky, Aske and Repple left with Rose and the Doctor in the drawing room.

'I make no pretence that this will be easy, gentlemen, Miss Tyler,' Oblonsky declared. His accented voice was slightly slurred by the wine and port. 'It will be a long and difficult process and we are by no means ready to embark on a full-scale reinvasion of the motherland.'

Sir George nodded and clapped a friendly hand on the colonel's shoulder. 'We are under no illusions,' he agreed. 'I believe young Freddie will have reached maturity before we can help him reclaim his birthright.'

'They've no hope, have they, Doctor?' Rose said quietly as they stood at the other end of the room, admiring a dark portrait of a serious lady.

'None,' he replied. He sounded genuinely sad. 'But it's good to dream. They're doing no harm.'

'What about the attack on Dickson?'

'Something else entirely, I think.' He frowned back at the woman in the picture. 'Dunno what, though.'

At the other end of the room, Repple and Oblonsky were deep in serious conversation. Aske drew Sir George to one side, closer to the Doctor and Rose. She heard him say, 'I wonder, Sir George, if you could spare me a few moments alone. There is something I wish to speak to you about. It is…' He paused and glanced over at Repple and Oblonsky. 'It is somewhat delicate.'

'The library?' Sir George suggested. The two men each nodded politely to the Doctor and Rose as they left.

Dickson had returned and was collecting empty glasses. The Doctor stopped him as he passed.

'Sir?'

'This evening – tell us again exactly what happened. As much detail as you can.'

If he was surprised or unwilling, he gave no sign. 'I heard a strange sound, saw a light coming from the yard. So I went to look.'

'Then what?' Rose asked.

He shrugged. 'A hand grabbed me from behind. Clamped over my mouth, turning me round. Then another hand was on my throat. It was cold, I remember. Very cold.'

'Cold as metal,' the Doctor murmured.

Dickson nodded. 'I struggled, but they were too strong. I could not break away. Then there was a voice, quiet, almost melodic…' He frowned into the distance as he remembered. 'Telling me that I had to answer questions. It asked me about Sir George and the guests due this evening, but before I could reply you came along.' He shrugged and took the glass the Doctor offered.

'Nothing else? No small detail you might've overlooked?'

'There was something odd, yes. A sound.'

The door opened again before he could go on. Sir George was looking grave, Aske apologetic, as they returned.

'I do understand,' Sir George said as they crossed the room. 'Unfortunate, but it cannot be helped.'

'You are very kind, sir,' Aske replied. 'Of course, anything we *can* do to help…'

'It is time we were going,' Repple announced.

Colonel Oblonsky saluted and Repple nodded in acknowledgement.

'Doctor, Miss Tyler,' Repple said as he came over, 'it is a short walk to the Imperial Club. Or we can call for a car if you would rather.'

'Short walk sounds great,' the Doctor said. 'I'll get my coat.' He froze, midway to the door. 'You hear that?'

'What?' Sir George asked, cocking his head to one side.

'I thought…' The Doctor frowned. 'Yeah, there it is again. Ticking.'

Rose could hear it too, now that the Doctor mentioned it. A low, dull clicking, barely audible. 'It's a clock,' she said.

'There is no clock,' Colonel Oblonsky replied quietly.

'That's right,' Sir George agreed. 'No clocks in the drawing room. There was one. It broke.' He shrugged, apologetically. 'Can't hear anything myself.'

'It's very quiet,' the Doctor said.

Aske and Repple exchanged looks. Both shrugged, not convinced.

But Dickson was standing alert and still. 'That's it, sir,' he said, his voice a hoarse whisper. 'That's what I heard. When I was attacked.'

'Must be coming from the hall,' Sir George said. 'There's the grandfather out there.'

'The hall,' the Doctor murmured, 'of course.' He put his finger to his lips, and went quickly and quietly to the door. He paused a moment, then yanked it suddenly open.

There was no one there.

'Tempus fugit,' the Doctor said.

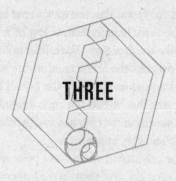

THREE

The Doctor, typically, was more concerned about finding his jacket than the fact someone might have been listening at the door. Despite Dickson's assurances that he would ask the staff in the morning and he was sure it would turn up, the Doctor was quiet.

He walked the mile through the cold dark streets with his arms folded and a vanilla expression on his face. He said almost nothing. Rose offered to lend him her cloak, but she told her not to be daft.

'I'm not cold. It's the principle.' Bizarrely, he was also more upset about his jacket disappearing from the dining room than he had seemed at the loss of the TARDIS, though it might be some sort of displaced anxiety. And his sonic screwdriver was in the pocket. But Rose was with Dickson, who reckoned someone had simply tidied it away and the thing would turn up in the morning. Sir George, apologetic and polite, promised to have it sent over as soon as it was found.

But the net result was that the walk to the Imperial Club was rather subdued. Repple seemed lost in a world of his own, rather like the Doctor. Aske talked politely to Rose, wondering how well she knew London. He seemed interested to hear that she was going to the British Empire Exhibition, confessing that he had not been himself, but several of the people staying at the club had and proclaimed it to be a great success and very impressive.

The Doctor brightened when Aske pointed out a large, imposing building ahead of them as the Imperial Club.

'We have to be members?' he wondered.

'I shall vouch for you,' Repple announced.

'The club was established after the Great War as a focal point, a meeting place, for the dispossessed nobility of Europe and the Commonwealth,' Aske said. 'So many things ended in Flanders, not just here and in France and Germany but right across the world.'

'So many lives,' the Doctor reminded him quietly.

Aske nodded grimly, one hand thrust deep in his jacket pocket. 'The ultimate sacrifice.'

'Such a waste,' Repple added. 'And it precipitated so much more. The Russian Revolution, for example. There will be so much more blood before all this is ended.'

'To answer your question, Doctor, you do not have to be members,' Aske said. 'Though if you desire to stay for more than a few days, then you will be expected to provide evidence that you are of noble birth, dispossessed by conflict.'

The Doctor nodded, sombre again for a moment. 'Anything's possible,' he murmured, staring into the distance.

'The Great War.'

'So who runs this place?' Rose wanted to know as Repple led them up the steps to the imposing double doors.

The doors opened for them, and a man in a smart doorman's uniform saluted. Repple nodded, and Aske saluted in return. The Doctor smiled and waved his hand in acknowledgement.

'Cheers,' Rose said.

The doorman closed the doors behind them, and took their coats.

'I don't have one,' the Doctor said glumly.

'Very good, sir,' the doorman replied.

'No, it's not.'

Aske caught the doorman's attention before the Doctor could continue. 'Is Mr Wyse still up?'

'You'll find him in the Bastille Room, sir.'

'Wyse runs the place, in effect,' Aske explained as he led them through the large foyer. Marble columns rose up to a vaulted roof, and a wide stone staircase curved up to the floors above. There were several corridors off from the entrance hall, all of them panelled with dark wood and hung with paintings and pictures. The corridor he led them through was decorated with woodcuts and watercolours depicting events of the French Revolution.

The Doctor paused to inspect one of the pictures. 'That's not right,' he told Rose. But he moved on without elaborating.

'Wyse is a resident here,' Aske was saying. 'I'm not sure exactly what his status is, but the staff seem to defer to him.'

They emerged into an enormous room. The wooden

panelling continued round the walls to shoulder height, making it seem very dark, despite the many wall lights. A chandelier hung down in the middle of the room, sparkling like a cluster of stars in the night sky. A large fire crackled and spat in an enormous stone fireplace, on the opposite wall to the door they had come in by. Leather armchairs and small leather sofas were arranged round low tables so that each of the many seating areas was an island in the large room. At first glance the place seemed empty.

Then a head appeared round the back of one of the armchairs. A hand waved. 'Evening to you,' a cheery voice called. 'Care to join me for a nightcap or whatever?' The head disappeared, and a moment later the man had got to his feet and emerged from the other side of the chair.

He was a tall, well-built man in his mid-forties with short brown hair that could have been better behaved. Like Aske and Repple, he was dressed in a dark suit. Unlike them, and to Rose's amusement, he was wearing a monocle. She hoped he would do that thing where the monocle fell out and dangled on a chain. But, to her disappointment, he pushed it firmly into place and regarded them all with interest.

'Well, what have we here?' the man declared as he looked at the Doctor and Rose. 'More refugees from the palaces and mansions of Europe, or just a couple of visitors, what?'

'You must be Mr Wyse,' the Doctor decided, striding through the furniture to shake his outstretched hand.

'Lord Wyse as a point of actual fact. But we don't stand on ceremony, dear me no. Just Wyse will do very nicely, thankee. Too many people like Repple here have lost too much for those of us with anything left to flaunt it in their faces.' He gestured for them to sit down. Rose saw that there was a chess set on a board on the table in front of where Wyse had been sitting, in the middle of a game.

'Oh, ignore my rather inept attempt to beat meself at chess, won't you?' Wyse said, smiling, and to Rose's ill-concealed delight the monocle did pop out of his eye and swing on a thin chain. 'And shift that dratted cat out of the way. Old Hector was sitting there earlier, and I think the thing likes the residual warmth.'

The cat that was stretched out on the sofa blinked its eyes open at the noise. It rolled on to its back and Rose watched its claws extend, curl, then retract as it yawned. It was a black cat, with a pale triangle of lighter fur under its chin. She reached down and stroked the pale fur, and was rewarded with a purr and the intense stare of the cat's deep glassy eyes. After a moment it stretched again, then leaped down from the sofa and slunk off under the chair where Wyse had sat himself down again.

'What's its name?' Rose asked.

'Oh dear, you've got me there.' Wyse smiled. 'Just call it "the cat" meself. Been here longer than I have, that cat. But speaking of names…'

'I'm Rose. This is the Doctor.'

'Hi,' the Doctor said, slumping himself down where the cat had been. 'We're told you're the man to ask about a room for the night. Maybe two nights.'

Wyse laughed. 'Nothing much to do with me, but I can put in a word if you think it will help. I've been here longer than anyone else, so when Mr Pooter's away they listen to me. I'll tell Crowther to make up a couple of rooms. Have to be on the third floor, mind. Pretty full at the moment, and we're not terribly big really, you know.'

'Mr Pooter,' Aske said, 'is the gentleman who endowed the club originally. It is run by a board of trustees that meets regularly. Mr Pooter is the chairman of that board.'

'Not here now, though,' Wyse said. 'He lives on the fourth floor, top of the building, and he likes his privacy. Bit of a recluse, I think. When he's not travelling. Likes his own company.'

'Yeah, don't we all,' the Doctor agreed.

'You all right, Repple?' Wyse asked, leaning forwards. Repple was sitting in the armchair opposite with his eyes closed. They opened slowly at Wyse's words, and he stared back at the other man.

'I have had a busy day,' he said. 'It's late.' His eyes closed again, and his head slipped to one side.

'Yes, you're looking a bit run down,' Wyse decided. 'I'll give him a hand getting to his room.'

'There's no need,' Aske said quickly.

'Oh, no trouble. You stay and talk to your friends here. I'll have Crowther let you know where their rooms are soon as they're ready.'

'Thanks.' Rose smiled at the man as he got up, and he grinned back.

He made a futile attempt to smooth down his hair. 'Goodnight to you then.' Wyse tapped Repple gently on the knee, and the eyes opened again. 'Come along, time to turn in, I think.'

Repple nodded, and Aske helped him up out of the chair. 'My apologies, Doctor, Miss Tyler,' Repple said. 'I just need some sleep. I shall see you perhaps for breakfast.'

Aske made to help Repple, but Wyse waved him away. 'It's no trouble.' He helped Repple across the room. The cat watched their progress all the way to the door, then it sprang to its feet and ran after them.

The Doctor was leaning forward, chin on his hands and elbows on his knees, looking at the chess game.

'Who's winning?' Rose asked.

'Since he is playing against himself, Wyse is winning.' He leaned back, hands clasped behind his head. 'Interesting.'

'Is he any good?'

'I'd say so.' The Doctor nodded, then turned towards Aske. 'Nice of you to bring us here.' He stood up abruptly and turned a full circle, inspecting the room before sitting down again. 'Yes, very nice indeed.'

'Is Repple all right?' Rose asked.

'He gets tired,' Aske said. 'Part of his condition, I'm afraid.'

The Doctor frowned. 'Condition?'

Aske nodded. He was looking pale and drained. 'I'm not sure quite how to explain, but I have a confession to make to you both. I'm afraid that things are not quite as they seem.'

The Doctor was fully attentive now, eyes focused sharply on Aske. 'Things are never quite as they seem.'

'Is this about Repple's condition?' Rose wondered.

Aske nodded. 'Tell me,' he said, fixing each of them in turn with his gaze, 'has either of you ever actually heard of

Dastaria?'

'No,' Rose admitted. 'But I'm rubbish at geography.'

'I'm rather good at it,' the Doctor retorted. 'But no. No, I haven't.'

This was obviously the answer Aske had expected. 'You have never heard of it, because there is no such place.'

'Playing his cards close to his chest, is he?' the Doctor said.

'You mean he didn't want us to know exactly where he is in exile from?' Rose said. If there really were assassins after him, then he would hardly advertise his presence, but why would he lie to the people who were supposed to be helping him?

Aske was still looking serious. 'It is more complicated than that.'

The Doctor nodded. 'Tell us, Major.'

Aske sighed. 'It isn't Major. In fact, like you, I am something of a doctor. I dabble in the new sciences of the mind, though I cannot pretend to be anything of an expert. I am no more a soldier than my friend Edward Repple is an exiled ruler.'

It took Rose a moment to work out what he was talking about. 'Hang on – are you saying he's not what he claims at all? He's going round saying he's ruler of this place that doesn't exist, what, to get freebie dinners and stuff?'

The Doctor was shaking his head. 'I think poor Repple doesn't know he's lying. Is that right?'

Aske nodded sadly. 'I thought it was a game at first. But it became so compulsive.' He sighed. 'I had better start at the beginning. You see, my friend was in a pageant, a show. Part of the Empire celebrations last year before the exhibition was opened. There was a parade, and he was playing the part of the Elector of Dastaria – a fictitious role, one he and I invented together for the occasion. I was his aide-de-camp, a major in the Dastarian army.'

Aske got to his feet, pacing up and down in front of the sofa, his shadow crossing and recrossing the half-played chess game, one hand in his jacket pocket. 'It was a hot day. We were there, in the full sun for hours. Repple fainted. That was all, or so I thought. But when he came round… Perhaps it was the fall from the horse, I don't know. In fact, this interest of mine in the science of the mind, it stems from that moment.' His eyes were moist as he looked at Rose, as if begging her to understand.

'His fiction became his reality,' the Doctor said.

'Yes. As I say, I thought he was playing the fool, having a joke with us. But no, he really believed – and still believes – himself to be the Elector of Dastaria. He has somehow rationalised the fact that he is in London and not ruling his country by assuming he has been deposed and is preparing to return in glory.'

'To a country that doesn't even exist,' Rose said. It was sad. 'And you haven't told him the truth?'

Aske gave a short bark of laughter, though it was empty of mirth. 'Oh, I have tried, Doctor. I have spent many hours trying to talk him out of this delusion. But without success. I thought it would be difficult to play along, but I have to confess it has been very easy, once I accepted we would have to move away from everything he knows, or rather knew.' He sighed. 'The trustees were happy to allow us rooms here, and Wyse has been most eloquent on our behalf. Both Repple and I have modest private incomes that more than cover the costs.'

'And you get invited to parties,' Rose added.

Aske looked embarrassed. 'Yes. Well. The evening was a little more complicated than I had expected. It seems that Sir George had already spoken with Repple about this Russian business. I knew nothing about it until tonight and Repple was already offering to help. Offering help he cannot give.'

'And that's what you wanted to talk to Sir George about,' Rose realised.

'You tell him everything?' the Doctor wondered.

'To my shame, no,' Aske confessed. 'I warned him merely that Repple's support in Dastaria is nowhere near as great as he hopes and expects and believes. That it is very unlikely he will be able to offer any material help at all. Sir George was disappointed, of course. But I'm afraid he still expects too much.'

'I wouldn't worry about that,' the Doctor reassured him. 'Chances of Sir George's little adventure getting to the point where he'd want Repple's help must be slim to nothing.'

'Yeah, no hope,' Rose agreed.

Aske seemed to brighten at this. 'You think so?'

'Don't worry about Sir George.'

Further discussion was interrupted by the arrival of a tall man with thinning grey hair. He stood in the doorway and coughed artificially.

'Ah, Crowther,' Aske said. 'I gather you are sorting out rooms for our new guests.'

Crowther's voice was abrupt and brittle. 'The rooms are ready. I shall be happy to show you to them.'

'Ta,' the Doctor said. 'And thank you,' he said to Aske.

'The least I could do.' He shuffled anxiously. 'Doctor, I have told few other people about this. You will…'

'Mum's the word,' the Doctor assured him.

Their rooms were next to each other, with a small lounge between that was reached from either room by a connecting door. Each had a small bathroom en suite, which the Doctor murmured was as unusual as it was welcome. The rooms reminded Rose of what you might get in a posh country-house hotel. Not that she had ever been to such a place, but the four-poster bed and the worn leather furniture reeked of expense and comfort. She had not realised how tired she was until she saw the bed.

Crowther showed them through the rooms, then handed them each a key. 'Just one thing, sir and madam,' he said in his dry voice.

'Just one?' The Doctor smiled.

Crowther ignored this. 'Mr Pooter's rooms are directly above you. I would request that you make as little unneces-sary noise as possible.'

'I thought Mr Pooter was away,' Rose said.

'Indeed. But he often returns at very short notice or unex-pectedly. We have a trustees' meeting coming up shortly.'

'No wild parties, Rose,' the Doctor warned. 'No raves or

binges or barn-dancing.'

'And of course, you will respect his privacy.'

'Of course,' Rose said. She was finding the man more than a little creepy and wished he'd just leave them. 'I thought he'd never go,' she whispered as soon as Crowther had left the Doctor's room.

'Never is a very long time,' the Doctor said.

They both flinched at the knock at the door.

'I think he heard you,' Rose said.

The Doctor raised his eyebrows, not convinced. He strode across the room and opened the door. Repple was standing there, and the Doctor motioned for him to come in. The black cat slipped in behind him, before the Doctor could close the door. It stretched out on the floor inside the door and watched them.

The Doctor shrugged, and left the door open. 'Feeling better?' he asked.

'I had to speak to you,' Repple said. He looked round, as if checking there were only the three of them there. 'Even now he may be listening. Somewhere, somehow. I pretended to be tired, so as to get away, just for a few minutes.'

'From Major Aske?'

Repple nodded. 'I'm sorry,' he said, looking from the Doctor to Rose, 'but I have not been entirely honest with you.'

'There's a thing,' Rose muttered.

'You mean,' the Doctor said brightly, 'you're not actually the rightful leader of Dastaria?'

Repple stared at them, his expression not changing. He

seemed about to speak, but then there was a sound from outside. A gentle thud – like the wind blowing a window shut, or a door closing distantly on another floor. Or a furtive footfall.

'I misled you in some details,' Repple said quietly, glancing again over his shoulder. 'I am not the Elector of Dastaria, exiled and even now planning my glorious return to power.'

The Doctor looked at Rose and raised an eyebrow in an 'I told you so' way.

'What?' she retorted.

Repple seemed not to notice. 'I cannot begin to plan my return, glorious or otherwise. You see, the truth is, I am a prisoner in all but name.'

'Hang about,' Rose said. 'Are you the ruler of this place or not?'

'I am. But as you know, I was deposed in an illegal coup. The rebels seized power without any warning or legitimacy. And one day I shall reclaim my title. But first, I must escape.'

'Escape?'

'From him. From Aske – my jailer.'

'Ah.' The Doctor made it sound as if everything was now clear, but he mouthed 'Eh?!' at Rose.

Repple turned away. 'He watches me all the time. Only occasionally, like now, can I slip away for a few moments. But I must get back, before he becomes suspicious. I can plan nothing, talk to no one without him knowing. And if I step out of line for a moment, if he even begins to think I have violated the terms of my exile...' He shook his head at the thought. 'The man is a fanatic.'

'Yes,' the Doctor said slowly, 'I'm sure.'

'But what can he do?' Rose demanded.

'You have noticed how he stands?' Repple demonstrated, mimicking Aske's distinctive posture – one hand tucked into his jacket pocket. 'A knife or a small pistol is never far away. I can take no chances. Not for myself, you understand. I do not fear death.' He looked from Rose to the Doctor. 'I fear for my people. Those left behind in the country that despite everything still flies our flag.'

'Course you do,' the Doctor said, clapping his arm round Repple's shoulder. 'So, what's the flag of Dastaria look like?'

Was he trying to catch the man out, Rose wondered? If so, it did not seem to work. Repple answered immediately. 'It is a white triangle emblazoned on a background of the night sky. And one day soon, despite what Aske and those he answers to might think, I shall return in glory at the head of an army that marches under that flag. For freedom. For Dastaria.' He stepped away from the Doctor, regarded him for a moment, then enfolded him in an embrace. Rose stepped quickly out of range. But Repple made no attempt to give her the same treatment. Instead he clicked his heels together and bowed in her direction. 'There is a degree of honour in you both,' he said. 'I know I can count on you.'

Then, with a curt nod, he turned and walked from the room.

The cat turned lazily without getting up and watched him go. Then it turned back towards Rose, and she gasped as she noticed its neck. A white triangle on its black fur.

'Doctor – look. The markings on the cat.'

'Yeah. Could be a coincidence.'

'Or,' Rose said, completing both their thoughts, 'could be that's where he got the idea for the design of the flag. If he's making it up.'

'Trouble is,' the Doctor said, 'it could be where he got it even if he's not making it up. A subconscious image.'

'Is he lying? And if he is, does he know it?'

'And if he isn't, why is Aske lying?' The Doctor tapped his index finger against his teeth. 'Curiouser and curiouser. Know what we need?'

Rose nodded. 'A good night's sleep followed by a hearty breakfast.'

'Spot on. See you in the morning.' He nodded at their feline visitor, still stretched out on the carpet. 'And knowing what curiosity did…'

Rose grinned. 'Yes, you'd better put the cat out.'

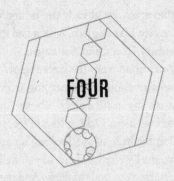

FOUR

The view from the Doctor's window was of an icy morning in London. If he leaned out, breathing in the crisp air, he could see the Palace of Westminster. He could not actually see the icicles hanging from the clock face of Big Ben, as the clock tower at the Houses of Parliament was popularly called. But he could imagine them – slivers of frozen glass, glistening in the early light as the first drips thawed and rolled and fell from the ends.

Beside the Palace of Westminster was the calm, gunmetal-grey surface of the Thames. He noted the position where the Millennium Wheel was conspicuous by its absence, and smiled at his memories of what was yet to come. Apart from the wheel, the general shape of the skyline would not change that much. Lower down it would – among the glass and concrete and neon that was not yet built. But the general impression of London, what made it instantly recognisable, was already set. With the addition of Tower Bridge, the image was complete. It had been there less than thirty-five years, yet already the bridge was a timeless emblem of the city. Like Big Ben, which had itself been there less than a century. Iconic and distinctive.

Anyone looking up from the street below would see the Doctor's head and shoulders emerging from his window. His chin was resting in his hands, elbows on the wide sill. The eyes were ever alert, flicking to and fro, taking in every last detail. One might imagine, looking up and discovering him there, that the Doctor had been like this all night. Frozen like an icicle, staring out and thinking. And perhaps he had.

But now he moved. Straightening up and withdrawing inside, the Doctor blew on his pale, cold hands and rubbed them vigorously together. It was morning, he could hear the distant sounds of the docks and the clatter of traffic in the street. London was waking, even if Rose was not. It was time to get started, time to get some answers, time for breakfast.

The first Rose knew of morning was when the door opened. She grunted something incoherent as she disentangled her head from the heavy blankets and sheet. It was meant to be 'Go away', but evidently it hadn't come out like that as someone had come into the room.

Rose grabbed the blankets and pulled them up again, retreating. They seemed to separate and go everywhere – didn't they have duvets? Her gran used to call a duvet a 'continental quilt' so maybe convenience bedlinen had only got as far as France. She peeped over the sheet, and saw that there was a girl of about her own age or younger standing in the doorway. She had a bob of dark hair and a round face with a dot of a nose and wide brown eyes. She was wearing a dark uniform with a white apron.

'Oh, I do beg your pardon, miss.' The girl curtsied awkwardly, as embarrassed as Rose was. 'The gentleman said it was all right to make up the beds and do the rooms, I didn't realise you was still asleep.'

'I wasn't,' Rose lied. 'Come in, it's fine,' she decided. Trust the Doctor to get the maid to wake her. Or maybe he'd just forgotten she existed. Typical.

'I couldn't do that.' The girl looked pale at the thought.

'Don't be daft. It's time I got up.'

The girl's name was Beth, and once she had got over the embarrassment she was quite chatty. Rose bombarded her with questions about the Imperial Club, but learned little more than she already knew. Getting dressed in her one and only set of clothes, Rose asked about where to go shopping for more. She hoped the Doctor had some cash that worked here – she couldn't see any of the rather staid-sounding shops that Beth suggested taking Galactic Express Gold Card or whatever.

'How long have you worked here?' Rose wondered, sitting on the newly made bed and swinging her legs so that her pale-green dress seemed to blow out around her.

'Oh, I've been in service for five years now.'

'Five years?' She must be older than she looked, Rose thought. But she was wrong.

'Yes, I started at Lord and Lady Hutchinson's when I was fourteen. Had a poky little room under the eaves. This time of year it was perishing, it was.'

'Isn't that a bit young?'

'Oh, not really, miss. And me mum needed the money. I send home half my pay every week. I got two younger brothers and a sister, you see. So it all helps.'

Rose nodded. 'I suppose.' She could recall Gwyneth at the undertaker's in Cardiff had gone into 'service' when very young. Clearly things hadn't exactly moved on since the end of the last century.

'I'm glad I live in here, though,' Beth went on. 'We all have rooms in the other wing. Not allowed through here except when we're working, you see. Mr Crowther would have a fit if he caught us loitering about with nothing to do. But what with the rumours and everything, I don't go out more than I have to.'

'Rumours?'

'They say there's someone going about attacking people in service round here. Old Mrs Fewsham's maid was approached the other week by a stranger in a dark street and she fainted clean away. Mind you,' Beth said, thinking about it, 'she's like that. But then there was Mary from the Lawrences'. Week in hospital she got, and she can still barely talk. Says it was something horrible.'

'She can manage a bit then,' Rose murmured.

'Shadowy figures reaching for your throat and asking questions about the other staff and who you work for...' She shuddered at the idea. 'Don't bear thinking about.'

Rose shuddered too as she recalled the events of the previous evening – the shadowy figure and the marks on Dickson's neck. 'No,' she agreed. 'It don't.' It was time she got some food. Maybe the Doctor would have saved her a bacon sandwich. 'I'll leave you to do the Doctor's room,' she told Beth.

'Oh, I've been in there already, miss,' Beth admitted. 'But there weren't much to do. The bed's not been slept in.'

Breakfast was long gone, and the Doctor seemed more amused than sympathetic. He was sitting in the panelled room playing chess with Wyse. He had a finger raised in the air for silence even before Rose saw him, but she had no doubt it was for her benefit.

She slumped down on one of the leather chairs in the otherwise deserted room and watched as the Doctor mulled over various moves. A slight movement at the edge of her vision made her turn, and she saw that the cat was lying on the adjacent sofa. It raised its lazy head and regarded her with interest for a moment. But only a moment, then it lowered its head again and seemed to go to sleep.

Rose kissed the air in the cat's direction encouragingly. The Doctor spared her a glare, and she stopped. 'Sorry,' she muttered just loud enough for him to hear, though he ignored it.

Wyse caught Rose's eye, and winked. 'Think I've got him on the run,' he whispered.

The Doctor looked up at them, eyes narrowed. Then he returned his attention to the board. 'Oh, stuff it,' he decided, and moved a bishop forwards.

Wyse frowned. 'Or not,' he admitted.

'Breakfast?' Rose asked.

'Was great,' the Doctor told her. 'Bad luck.' He tapped the edge of the chessboard. 'Mate in three,' he finished glumly.

Wyse nodded. 'I'll find Crowther and have him get you some bacon and eggs,' he said to Rose.

'Thanks. But why not stay and finish him off first? If it's only three moves.'

Wyse smiled sadly. 'I'm afraid it's three moves until he finishes me off. Brilliant move there with the bishop, I have to say.' He stood up and stretched. 'Right then, back in a tick.'

The cat mirrored Wyse's movements, stretching, getting to its feet and walking from the room in its long, easy manner.

'Having fun?' Rose asked.

The Doctor grinned. 'Yeah. Takes my mind off faceless killers and missing time machines. He's very good,' he went on, picking up Wyse's black king and examining it.

'Not up to your standard, though.'

'I dunno.' He put the king back, laying it on its side. 'He missed an easy way to beat me early on.'

'Giving you a chance?'

'I wonder. P'raps he felt sorry for me. I was going to return the favour just now, but I couldn't see a move that didn't leave my king exposed.'

'Except winning.'

'Winning's easy.'

'So, maybe he forced you to win.'

The Doctor considered this. 'Which is lots more difficult,' he decided quietly.

* * *

The chief steward, or whatever Crowther was, brought through a tray of breakfast for Rose. If he disapproved of her eating it off her lap, he said nothing. Rose couldn't believe how much she had missed bacon – something so simple, yet her mouth was watering in anticipation just at the smell as she lifted the silver lid from her plate. The poached egg looked good too, but she gave the black pudding a miss. There was toast, and a pot of tea, and cups for all three of them on another tray, brought by an unsmiling maid who seemed barely older than Beth.

'It's a rum do,' Wyse said when Rose mentioned the attacks that Beth had told her about. 'Don't seem to be any call for it. No clear motive. Very sad.' He shook his head. 'Repple was saying something about Sir George Harding's man being attacked last night, right outside his house. Terrible, terrible.'

'We were there,' Rose admitted through a mouthful of toast.

'Or perhaps it was Aske,' Wyse went on. 'Don't remember offhand.' He looked up, as if realising what Rose had said. 'You were there?'

'No big deal,' she assured him. 'Saved the good guy, fought off the baddies. The usual, you know.'

The Doctor was setting up the chessboard again. 'How many attacks have there been?'

Wyse was staring at Rose, surprised at her dismissive attitude. 'Six or seven, I suppose. That we know about, anyway. One fatality, otherwise men in service just rather frightened and shaken up. Even a couple of women, one scarcely more than a girl, poor thing. You wonder what the world is coming to sometimes, don't you?'

Rose glanced at the Doctor, smiling at the fact that they did not need to wonder, they knew. The Doctor smiled back. But it was fleeting, gone in a moment. 'What was Repple's interest?' he wondered.

'Or Aske's,' Wyse said. 'Those two are like those Shakespearean characters, Rosencrantz and Guildenstern. Can't always tell them apart. Or maybe I mean Hamlet and Horatio,' he decided. 'Got to remember the royalty aspect.' He leaned forward, grinning suddenly, and gave a huge wink.

'You're winking at me,' the Doctor said.

'Er, yes. S'pose I am.'

'So I assume Aske has told you that Repple isn't really the king in exile or whatever.'

Wyse sat back in his chair and regarded them both with interest. 'He has indeed. He tells everyone that, then swears them to secrecy. Just as Repple tells everyone he is indeed the rightful Elector of Dastaria.'

'But which of them is telling the truth?' Rose asked. 'Repple told us he's a prisoner.'

'Tell me,' Wyse said, 'was Aske listening when he told you this?'

'Is that important?'

'Oh yes, Doctor. You wanted to know which of them had told you the truth.'

'Yep.'

'Well, it sounds as if the answer is: neither of them.'

'So what is the truth?' Rose put the cover back on her

plate – empty save for the slices of black pudding – and set down the tray on the table beside the chessboard.

'An excellent question, my dear. And I relate only what has been told to me, so I cannot directly vouch for its veracity either.'

'Get on with it,' the Doctor mumbled.

Wyse smiled affably at the interruption. 'Very well, my friend. Now, I asked if Repple believed he could be overheard when he told you his story. I know from the story he chose to tell that the answer is yes.'

Rose nodded. 'He seemed to be going to tell us something last night, then there was a noise and he got nervous.'

'You mean his story varies depending who's listening?' the Doctor said.

'Something like that.'

'So is he or isn't he?' Rose demanded.

'That is the question,' Wyse agreed. 'And no, I'm afraid he isn't.' As he spoke, the cat jumped up into Wyse's lap. It purred contentedly, snuggling in and almost immediately going to sleep. Wyse rubbed at the cat's head with his knuckles.

'So Aske told us the truth. It's all a delusion,' Rose realised.

'Well, that's not quite true either. You see, it's no delusion. Repple is in perfect mental health and he knows full well that he is no more the Elector of Dastaria than you or I.'

'So why lie?' the Doctor asked.

'Because Aske is the one with the delusions, and Repple wants nothing more than to humour his friend and allow him to continue with the life he believes he is leading.'

'Aske said he was treating Repple. That he's his psychiatrist or whatever.'

Wyse nodded. 'And that is his delusion. Aske believes himself to be a brilliant doctor of the mind, treating a friend who suffers from terrible delusions brought about, if I recall the story correctly, by a fall from a horse.' He looked from Rose to the Doctor and back again. 'It isn't Repple who believes himself to be something he is not and is aided and abetted in this by his friend. It is Aske.'

With that, Wyse excused himself. 'Time is marching on,' he said, 'and so must I.' He set the cat down on the floor. It opened a surprised eye, watching Wyse as he left, then slinking off after him.

'Doesn't matter,' Rose decided when he had gone.

'What doesn't?'

'Aske and Repple. None of our business really.'

'Interesting though,' the Doctor countered. 'Aren't you curious to know the truth?'

'You don't think we just heard it?'

'He said himself, it's just hearsay. Maybe Dastaria does exist – some out-of-the-way country lost between the cracks on the maps. Who knows?'

'Who cares?' Rose responded.

The Doctor's response to that, if he had one, was interrupted by Crowther. He coughed politely as he arrived to take Rose's breakfast tray. 'Excuse me, Doctor, but you have a visitor.'

'Really? Who?'

'It is a Miss Heart. She says you met last evening, sir. I'm afraid that since she has not been vouched for by a full member of the club, as you and Miss Tyler have been, she is only permitted so far as the public gallery. If you would follow me?'

'You coming?'

'And play gooseberry to you and the Painted Lady?' Rose said. 'It's you she wants to see, not me.'

'Jealous?' the Doctor asked innocently.

'I'll wait here and finish my tea,' Rose said. 'Don't want to cramp your style.'

The Doctor grinned.

'Such as it is,' Rose finished.

The grin vanished. The Doctor leaned forward and took Rose's hand. 'It's you that needs the fashion tips,' he said. 'Come on.'

'Beth didn't say anything about someone being killed,' Rose told the Doctor as Crowther showed them into the public gallery, off the main foyer.

'Beth?'

'The maid. You remember, you sent her to wake me up.'

'Oh yeah. Beth.'

'People hospitalised, traumatised, all sorts of other "ised"s. But she never mentioned dead-ised.'

'P'raps Beth doesn't know.'

The room was long and narrow, barely more than a wide corridor. One side was almost entirely taken up with large windows, the other had paintings hanging the length of it.

Down the middle of the room were various pieces of sculpture. Nothing modern, Rose noted. There were classical women looking as if they'd just got out of the bath, and heroic male figures with muscles – and everything else – rippling.

Melissa Heart was standing just inside the door, her back to them. She was admiring one of the statues, a woman poised with one arm in the air. Long sheetlike robes were sculpted round her, seeming to emphasise rather than disguise the female form. There was an odd similarity with Melissa Heart, standing there in her long, thin dress. She held a long, thin black cigarette holder to her mouth, trails of smoke wafting up towards the ceiling.

Rose wondered what the woman looked like under the mask. She imagined she was about to find out as Melissa Heart turned. But she was not. It was difficult to tell whether she was wearing thick white make-up with stylised red swirls painted on it, or whether this was another thin, face-tight mask. But whichever it was, her true features were once again shrouded in mystery.

The position of two of the red curls, lifting from the edges of the mouth, made it seem as if the woman was perpetually smiling. 'Why, Doctor, and Rose. How kind of you to see me.'

'Yes,' the Doctor agreed simply.

'How can we help?' Rose asked.

'Oh, but you can't. At least, not just now. Not yet.' The emotionless mask continued to smile at them. 'But I can help you, I think.'

'Really?'

She gestured with the cigarette holder towards an upright chair standing against the wall close by. A dark leather jacket was draped over it. 'Yours, I believe.'

The Doctor all but leaped across the room and snatched up the jacket. He slipped it on. 'It fits!'

'I thought it might.'

'I mislaid it last night,' the Doctor said, his expression suddenly as unreadable as Melissa's.

'I had reason to call on Lady Anna this morning, and she asked if I would return it to you. I confess, I did rather relish the chance to renew our acquaintance.'

'That's nice,' Rose said. She was rewarded with a brief glance from the blank face.

'You didn't happen to check the pockets, did you?' the Doctor said, rummaging inside them.

'Of course not.' Her voice too was devoid of expression.

'That's good.' He drew out the sonic screwdriver and held it up so she could see it clearly. 'Still, everything seems to be here.'

'How intriguing. What, may I ask is that?'

'Novelty corkscrew,' Rose told her.

'Or something,' the Doctor added. 'Found it in the street outside Sir George's. You don't know who might own such a thing?' He held out the sonic screwdriver, as if inviting her to take it.

'I really could not say.'

Melissa Heart reached out, but the Doctor pulled away his hand and slipped the device back into his jacket pocket. 'Thought not,' he said. 'Well, thanks. And bye.'

'We mustn't keep you,' Rose said. 'I expect you're busy.'

'Not at all.' If she was offended, there was no way of knowing. 'You must call on me some time. Both of you,' she added in a tone that implied she did not for one moment mean to include Rose. 'My house is not far away. Perhaps you know it? Anthony Hubbard's old house on Veracity Avenue.'

'We don't,' Rose said. 'We've not been here long.'

'You are travelling together?'

'We're inseparable,' the Doctor said.

'Then I shall leave you together. No doubt I shall see you again soon.'

'No doubt,' the Doctor echoed. 'Thanks for the coat. I must call in and thank Sir George and his wife as well.'

Melissa Heart hesitated. Only slightly, but enough for Rose to notice. She knew it would not have escaped the Doctor.

'I'm sure there's no need,' Melissa said, pausing in the doorway.

'I'm sure you're right,' the Doctor agreed. Because now they all knew that however Melissa Heart had got the Doctor's coat, it was not from Sir George or his wife.

'It is all circumstantial. The sonic device, the detected power, the fact they are always together.' Melissa Heart sighed behind her mask. The dark figure sitting beside her in the car did not reply. Her fingertips stroked down the pale surface of her mask. 'Damning, but not conclusive. Not yet. And I must be sure. To go through this, to suffer... And innocent people have died. Too many people. I cannot be responsible for more.'

Her eyes were burning behind the mask as she studied her companion's equally blank face. 'We need to be absolutely sure. There is a maid called Beth. I heard the girl say she spoke with her. This maid may know something. May even know which of them it is. I have a description from one of the other staff.' It had been easy to get – the pretence of a friend for whom Beth had worked. Was it the same girl – what did she look like? When did she finish for the day? So very easy.

The blank-faced figure listened to its instructions. It said nothing, and when Melissa Heart had finished, it bowed its head slightly in acknowledgement. As it moved, the staccato clicking of its mechanism was like the ticking of a clock.

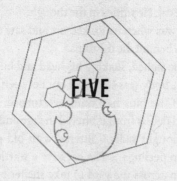

FIVE

A brisk walk had cleared the cobwebs from Wyse's mind. He liked to walk through the familiar landscape of London. There was a faint mist in the air, the beginnings of a smoggy day to come. His breath came in brisk clouds of its own as he walked back towards the Imperial Club, his gloved hands clasped tightly behind his back and his head down in thought.

He was being followed, of course – he knew and accepted that. He ignored it, and concentrated on more urgent and immediate matters. But even these were sent scurrying from his mind when he saw the body.

Wyse had taken a shortcut down a back alley round to the rear of the club. The alley opened into a yard behind the building. The various staff came and went through the back entrance, so as not to have to go through the main members' areas. Wyse counted himself as almost staff. He was on first-name terms with them all. He had been here longer than any of them, even longer – just – than Repple and Aske.

Him and the cat. He smiled at the thought.

And that was when he looked up, and saw the legs sticking out from behind the dustbins.

'Oh no,' he sighed, shaking his head and hurrying across the yard. The body was stretched out between dustbins and wall. One of the bins had been overturned, perhaps in a struggle, and debris from it littered the ground. What a way to die, he thought sadly – littered with old papers, apple cores, potato peelings… The cat gave a startled hiss at the sight and ran across the yard to take shelter by the door to the club.

'Crowther!' Wyse yelled. 'Anyone! Quickly, I need some help here.' But he knew that wasn't true. Beth was dead, he could see that – her throat crushed and bruised and her eyes staring up blankly at the clouds. Wyse reached out and closed them gently. He could hear the thump of running feet, the gasped comments and questions. 'So close,' he murmured. 'So close to the club.'

'Oh my…' The usually unruffled Crowther turned away, face as grey as his remaining hair, hand to mouth.

'Get a doctor,' Wyse said. 'No,' he decided. 'Get the Doctor.' If anyone could tell what was really going on here, the Doctor could.

They sat in their usual little island of chairs and sofas by the table with the chess set. Rose was pale and quiet, the image of the dead girl still imprinted on her mind. Beth's voice and nervous laughter still echoing in her ears.

The Doctor and Wyse were talking quietly but urgently.

The Doctor had quickly examined the body, reminding them he was not a doctor of medicine. Even so, he was sure that the girl had been dead for an hour at most, probably a lot less. The marks on her neck were like the marks on Dickson's the night before. But deeper, darker, and more damaging.

'Have you any idea what is happening here?' Wyse asked.

'You think I might?'

Wyse shrugged. He looked old and drawn, as if finding the girl's body had sapped some of the life from him too. 'You seem like a man with insight. This has to be stopped. A few attacks, the odd person knocked out… Well, that's bad enough, of course. But, Doctor, a girl has died. Out there behind this club. On our very doorstep.' He took a long, deep breath. 'We cannot just sit by and do nothing.'

'The police,' Rose said, looking up for the first time. 'They'll…'

'They'll do their best,' Wyse said. 'But do any of us really think that will be good enough?' He turned to the Doctor, looking straight into his eyes. 'Do you know something, Doctor? Anything? About all this?'

The Doctor held his gaze for several moments. Then he stood up, hand to forehead, sighing and sad. 'Enough. I know an innocent girl's dead. I know whoever – whatever – did this has to be stopped. That's enough.'

'And what do you propose, Doctor?'

The Doctor sat down again, leaning forward from the edge of the chair. 'There's more to this than we know or guess. And you,' he pointed at Rose, 'need a distraction. It's terrible and brutal and unfair, but moping won't help.'

'I like moping. When people get killed.'

'We need to be alert, aware, sparking with ideas.'

'Fat chance.'

'And I still want to see the British Empire Exhibition.'

'Ah!' Wyse perked up at this. 'It's very good actually. Lots on, you know. And the new stadium is a glory to behold.'

'You go then,' Rose told him, looking away.

'Oh, I've been. I'd welcome the chance to go again, mind. But I fear the police will want to take a statement from me.'

'From you?' Rose frowned, looking at him.

'He did find the body,' the Doctor pointed out.

'Oh. Yeah.'

'I reckon we should avoid making statements,' the Doctor went on, looking meaningfully at Rose. 'It'd only confuse them.'

'You'll enjoy the exhibition,' Wyse said gently. 'I would like to join you, but I expect they'll delight in keeping me hanging around for a while just to demonstrate how important they are. The Doctor's right, my dear. It'll take your mind off things.'

Rose didn't like being called 'my dear'. But somehow coming from Wyse in such a disingenuous manner, it seemed friendly and kind rather than patronising. 'OK,' she said.

'Triffic!' The Doctor clapped his hands together and leaped to his feet. 'You get your cloak, and I've already got my jacket back.' He paused, lips pursed as he thought. 'Let's call in on Sir George on the way and thank him for returning it.'

'Except you know he didn't.'

'We ought to be sure,' he said. 'Or we're being unfair too.'

Rose sighed. 'I suppose. Hey,' she thought suddenly, 'I wonder if Freddie wants to come to the show. I doubt he gets out much.'

'That's true enough,' Wyse agreed. 'Poor little fellow.'

'Let's ask,' the Doctor said. 'Come on.'

The only hint Dickson gave that he had ever even seen the Doctor or Rose before was a slight widening of his eyes. He seemed to have completely recovered from his ordeal of the previous evening, deigning to acknowledge this with a neutral, 'Very well, thank you,' in response to Rose's enquiry.

'If you will wait in the drawing room, I'll see if Sir George is at home.'

'You'd think he'd know,' Rose said as Dickson marched off stiffly down the hall. She poked her head round the drawing-room door to watch him go.

'He knows. He's asking if Sir George wants to see us,' the Doctor replied from inside the room.

Rose turned to join him. But as she did, she caught sight of something moving through the balusters on the landing above. It reminded her of when they were leaving the night before, and she could guess what it was. Or rather, who.

'Hi, Freddie,' she called.

'Hello,' he replied, a little sheepishly. He stood up and looked down at her over the rail. 'Have you come back for the coat?'

'I've got it back.' The Doctor was beside Rose in the

hallway now. He opened his jacket and jiggled it, just to prove he was telling the truth. 'See. Why don't you come down and join us for a minute?' Freddie hesitated. 'Come on, it's you we've come to see, really.'

Making up his mind, Freddie made his unsteady way down the stairs. He did not have his crutch with him, but held tight to the railing all the way down. He dragged one leg slightly as he walked stiffly across the hall, but otherwise there was nothing to suggest he had trouble walking.

The Doctor led them into the drawing room. 'Yes, the kind Miss Heart brought my coat back,' he said.

'I saw her with it,' Freddie said, sitting down and giving a quiet sigh of relief. 'I saw…' He frowned and paused. 'I heard… lots of things,' he finished. He looked at Rose, his eyes moist. 'Is it true?'

'You listened to the grown-ups last night?' the Doctor asked.

Freddie nodded.

'Some of it's true,' Rose said.

'What Father said about me? About being the real Tsar?'

'Didn't you know?' Rose asked.

Freddie shook his head. 'No. Maybe. I don't remember.'

'What *do* you remember?' the Doctor asked. His tone suggested he was just making conversation, but Rose could see that he was staring intently at Freddie.

The boy looked away. 'It was a long time ago. I remember the boat, and meeting my new father for the first time. And I remember how happy Mother was to come to England. She cried.' He bit his lip at the memory. 'And I think

I remember my old father. He was nice and kind too. He had a big black beard, and he was always smiling. He carried me everywhere, so I wouldn't fall and hurt myself. And he said he would talk to the men outside the barn where we had to sleep that night. But then Mother said we had to go, we had to leave him behind. Mother carried me then, and that was nice. But I missed Father's soft voice and his strong arms.'

'When was this?' Rose wondered.

Freddie looked straight at her, his face pale. 'When Father shouted, and the men shouted too. When we heard the shooting.'

'Freddie.' The voice was quiet and calm and reassuring. 'Cook has made some cake.' Freddie's mother was standing just inside the doorway, and Rose wondered how much she had heard. 'Why don't you go and ask if you can have some?'

The boy grinned suddenly, and got to his feet. 'Thank you,' he said, walking stiffly across the room. He stopped in front of his mother.

She tousled his fair hair and smiled at him. But Rose could see too the sadness in her eyes. 'You'll be all right? You can manage?'

'Yes.'

'Go on then.'

She waited until the sound of Freddie's slow footsteps was gone before coming over to join the Doctor and Rose. 'I worry so much about him,' she said quietly. 'Even before, it was difficult. But when the revolution came, and Theo…' She shook her head. 'George has been so kind.' She blinked away the memories.

'It's been hard for you,' the Doctor said.

'Yes,' she said simply. 'I see you have recovered your coat, Doctor.'

He nodded. 'Yes, thanks. Melissa Heart said you asked her to return it to me.'

Anna frowned. 'Really? Well, perhaps Dickson found it and saw her. Sir George is working in his study, I'm afraid. He does not like to be disturbed, but if you wish to see him…'

'That's OK,' Rose said. 'We're off to the British Empire thingy.'

'Exhibition,' the Doctor explained as Anna looked confused.

'I have not been,' she confessed.

'That's all right.' The Doctor grinned. 'Not your empire, is it.' His grin froze. 'Sorry.'

'We wondered if Freddie wanted to come along,' Rose said quickly. 'He'd enjoy it.'

'I'm sure he would. You are very kind.'

From her tone, Rose could tell that the answer was no. 'You can come too. It'd make a nice day out.'

'A kind thought,' Anna said. 'But I would worry so much. He…' She paused, considering how to phrase what she wanted to say. 'It would not be safe for him, I fear.'

'I don't think there are assassins waiting round every corner,' the Doctor said.

'Assassins?' She frowned.

'He's just a boy,' Rose blurted out, suddenly upset and annoyed at the thought there might be people who wished him harm. Perhaps what had happened to Beth was somehow to do with Freddie. 'It's so unfair.'

'Unfair,' Anna agreed quietly. She bit her lip, just as Freddie had done a few minutes before, sitting in the same chair. Their expressions were almost identical, but years apart. 'Yes. So unfair.'

They sat in silence for a moment. Rose looked at the Doctor. The Doctor shrugged. Then Anna stood up and spoke.

'I shall ask Dickson to drive you to Wembley, if that is convenient.'

'Thanks,' the Doctor said.

'And Freddie may come with you in the car. But then Dickson will bring him straight home again. So that nothing happens to him.' She nodded, the decision made, though from her expression even this was not an easy choice to make. 'I really cannot allow him to wander about outside on his own. But he will enjoy the car journey. Thank you.'

'There's a kid in the block called Josh,' Rose said while they waited. 'His mum never lets him play out or anything. It's sad.'

'What's he like?' the Doctor asked.

Rose shrugged. 'No one knows. Quiet. Lonely.'

'Quiet ones rebel.'

'You'd know,' she teased. But he didn't answer.

The car was huge and noisy and black. All the cars, not that there were many, seemed to be black.

'Black is the old silver,' the Doctor told Rose when she pointed this out.

Freddie was excited. There were no seat belts, which worried Rose. What made her even more anxious was the way Freddie bounced on the leather seat as he stared out of the window, giving a running commentary on each and every little thing – interesting or not. The Doctor saw her watching anxiously, and shook his head – the boy was enjoying himself, and it didn't seem as if that happened often.

After about ten minutes, Freddie settled down as the novelty wore off. Rose was sitting next to him on the bench seat across the back of the car. The Doctor was opposite them on a seat that folded down from behind the driver, like in a cab. A glass screen separated them from Dickson in the front.

'It's strange seeing London with so few cars and people,' Rose said.

The Doctor nodded. 'More cars'll come soon enough.'

'And lots more women than men,' she realised.

'It's 1924,' the Doctor said, as if this explained it. 'There're about two million more women than men in Britain.'

Freddie nodded. 'Because of the war.'

'Of course,' Rose realised. 'That's why it's all so quiet.'

The Doctor leaned forward. 'That's why there are so few young men. The 1919 flu killed far more people than the Great War ever did.' He leaned back again, and closed his eyes. 'Whatever humanity inflicts on itself, nature can always go one better.' He opened his eyes again, but they were unfocused, as if staring at a different scene. Rose had to lean forwards herself to catch what he was saying: '…collapsed in the street. School children died at their desks between sums.'

'We're here,' Freddie said, his excited voice contrasting with the Doctor's sudden mood. The boy leaned across and took Rose's hand. 'You will tell me all about it, won't you?'

Rose smiled and squeezed his hand. 'Promise.'

It was massive: a city of classical buildings fashioned from grey concrete. A size and scale and sense of optimism that put the Millennium Dome to shame. Each and every country and dominion and colony of the British Empire was represented, some with their own vast concrete pavilions, some sharing with others.

Formal gardens and walkways meant that the mass of grey was never overpowering. Rose found it hard to credit that only eighty years before her time Britain still had an empire, although the Doctor explained it was more like the European Union – a collection of states and countries that in this case shared a common history rather than a common geography. But despite the fact that Britain no longer ruled many of them directly, there was a sense of cohesion and pride everywhere. In the enormous British government pavilion, a gigantic relief map of the world showed the extent of the empire. Even now, a quarter of the way through the twentieth century, that empire covered a quarter of the world.

It was both boring and fascinating in equal measure. Whenever they got tired of one thing, they simply moved on until something else caught their interest. They seemed to walk for miles. By late afternoon, as the light was fading and the crowds were thinning, Rose found it hard to distinguish between the different pavilions and exhibitions. She could remember grimacing at a collection of fox furs – silver, black, red and white – but could not recall whether they were from Canada or Newfoundland. Or Burma. She remembered both of them laughing at a field full of ostriches, but were they from South Africa or Tristan da Cunha? It was behind the full-size working replica of a diamond-washing plant, she knew that.

And it wasn't just the pavilions – each of them in the style of magnificent buildings in the country they represented. There was a South African train, where the Doctor and Rose were served sandwiches for lunch. There were flickering black-and-white films of local life in the various dominions and colonies. Tribal people from West Africa living in an exact replica of their own village at home, overshadowed by the concrete pavilion from India – its style reminiscent of the Taj Mahal.

There were sideshows and minor exhibits everywhere. In the Indian pavilion, it seemed as if every prince in that country had a stand where his staff were at pains to show off their ruler's achievements and the attractions of the local region.

'So nothing from Russia then,' Rose observed as they finally reached what seemed like the last few buildings.

'Nah – not part of the empire.'

'Got their own.'

The Doctor nodded. 'Yep. It'll last a while yet, though it's not in the greatest shape.'

'The revolution,' Rose said, thinking back to the discussions at Sir George's that first evening.

'Mmmm.'

'Not a great way to run an empire, I s'pose. Shooting the king or whatever.'

'The Tsar. And his wife. And his kids. No, not great... Mind you,' the Doctor added, 'Charles I got his head chopped off.'

'That was ages ago.'

'Which makes it better?' The Doctor clicked his tongue. 'Only ten minutes away in the TARDIS. Ends and means, always tricky.' He was looking round, as if trying to decide which way to go next. 'The women had diamonds sewn into their clothes. Bullets went whizzing round the room as they bounced off. Dead in a cellar,' he sighed, his breath misting the air. 'One of the most powerful families on the planet, and that's about the only thing people remember about them. That and haemophilia.' He seemed to have lost interest suddenly, and quickened his pace.

'Haemo-what?'

'Got it from Queen Victoria, something else people forget. It's a hereditary thing, stops the blood from clotting. The girls were fine, but poor little Alex had it. Nasty.'

Rose nodded, vague memories of a TV news item about exhuming the Tsar's family drifting back. 'Good job Charles I didn't have it then.'

The Doctor grinned back at her, and the past was the past again – something distant you could joke about, not a tragic memory. 'Like I said, it's the one thing people remember about the Romanovs. That and the fact they died.'

At the back of the vast exhibition area was an enormous

amusements park for the children. Here the variety and divergence of the lands of the empire made way for a full-size model of the old woman who lived in a shoe. There certainly were so many children that no one could have known what to do. But it seemed to Rose she hadn't actually been too hard done by – with all manner of games and amusements including a miniature railway to entertain her guests.

Freddie, she thought sadly, would have adored it. The place was like an innocent and naïve version of the theme parks Rose knew. Instead of roller coasters and rides, there were see-saws and swings and rocking horses. And instead of bored parents shouting at their children or ignoring them, there was an army of uniformed nurses supervising the youngsters so that parents could wander freely through the empire of reality while their children explored the wonders of this imaginary world.

'That's progress for you,' she thought.

But the biggest shock was the final building.

'Know where you are yet?' the Doctor asked, amused at Rose's expression as she realised what she was looking at. Union Jacks flew from the flagpoles on the two gleaming white towers. The whole magnificent edifice looked new and confident and as if it would stand for ever as a reminder of the temporary world the Doctor and Rose had just walked through.

'Wembley Stadium.'

'They call it the Empire Stadium,' the Doctor told her. 'Largest sports arena in the world. Bigger than the Colosseum.'

'I saw them pulling down the towers,' Rose said. 'On the telly.'

'It opened for the FA Cup final last year, 1923.'

She was standing in awe, looking up at the white concrete that seemed so strong and permanent. Remembering the indignity of its destruction. 'Who won?'

The Doctor stared at her in something approaching disbelief. 'Bolton Wanderers,' he said. 'Who else?' In the same tone of voice, he added, 'It wasn't just random, you know. Whoever took the TARDIS must have had a good reason. It's time we got this sorted.'

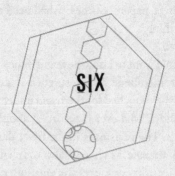

SIX

The building on the opposite side of the street was an imposing shadow in the gathering evening. Ronald Cheshunt sniffed and nodded as he watched the uniformed doorman walk slowly back and forth, gloved hands behind his back, feet stamping to keep warm.

'Never done a club before,' he confessed. 'You, Matty?'

Matty Black shook his head. He was a tall, lean man. A contrast to the rather shorter and more portly figure of Cheshunt. 'Looks easy enough.'

Cheshunt rubbed at his misshapen nose with a callused hand. 'Yeah. Easy. Tell us again what you're after.'

The woman remained in the darkest of shadows. The only good glimpse that Cheshunt had caught of her face had been a blank mask – literally. A smooth, paper-white approximation of a face made all the more disconcerting by the way her real eyes stared darkly out of it. 'Anything relating to the Doctor and Rose Tyler. You will search their rooms, now I have told you where they are. You will check their belongings, papers, clothes. I shall need a full description of everything.'

'Right. Yeah.'

'In addition, I want to know how and if they are registered as guests or members. What sureties if any they have offered. Who has vouched for them and under what circumstances. In short, whatever is recorded about them in the club's records. The register is in the front desk. The other records are in the safe, as I have told you. I shall also want to know of any security measures you encounter.'

'You what?' Cheshunt stared at the woman, his face almost as blank as hers.

A sigh from behind the mask. 'What precautions they have taken to deter intruders such as yourselves. Alarms, strong rooms, defences. Anything.'

'Oh, right.'

'There must be stuff more valuable than just papers and records,' Matty insisted. 'We'll come out of there laden,' he hissed excitedly to Cheshunt.

'You will not,' the woman said sharply. Her eyes glistened in the pale shape of the mask. 'You will confine yourselves to the matters I have specified. I would rather no one even knew you had been there.' She hesitated in the darkness, then went on, 'You may be wondering how I already know so much.'

'Your business.'

'True. But it may be of interest to you to know that an... associate of mine spoke to one of the staff at some length. I would have preferred to have her make further enquiries for me, but sadly she was not co-operative.'

'Yeah,' Matty said, not at all interested. 'Very sad.'

'My associate had to deal with her quite sternly.' She leaned forward and the glow from a nearby street lamp made her white face shine like a ghost. 'In fact, very sternly. As a result the unfortunate woman's services are no longer available to me. Or to anyone.' The face turned slowly from Cheshunt to Matty and back again. 'Do I make myself clear?'

Cheshunt could feel his heart thumping rhythmically in his chest as he realised what she was telling them. 'Very clear, lady. Very clear.' He nudged Matty with his elbow. 'We won't be taking nothing the lady don't want from inside. All right?'

Matty nodded, looking down at his feet as he shuffled nervously under the gaze of the faceless woman and the burly Cheshunt. If he saw the black cat stretched out in the shadows nearby, staring at them through startlingly green eyes, its ears pricked up attentively, he said nothing.

After they left the British Empire Exhibition, the Doctor and Rose took a cab back into the centre of London and went shopping. It was getting late, and the shops were beginning to close, but Rose still managed to find some clothes that she would feel more comfortable in. A woollen suit and a less frumpy dress were her main purchases. Jeans – or indeed any women's trousers – and T-shirts were nowhere to be found.

'Camouflage jackets are hard to find too,' the Doctor said.

Rose wasn't sure if he really wanted one or if he was joking. She didn't ask.

By the time she got back to the Imperial Club, Rose was exhausted. She and the Doctor ate dinner with Wyse, who was keen to hear all about their day. He nodded understandingly as they told him that Freddie had not been allowed to go to the exhibition. He seemed pleasantly surprised, though – as they had been – that Anna had let him come in the car. Rose pushed her food round the plate, too tired to eat much at all.

By the end of the meal, she could hardly keep her eyes open. The Doctor and Wyse were talking politics. Or something. Boring, whatever it was. She made her excuses and left them to it. The Doctor was obviously happy to continue his talk without Rose's help, though he was polite enough not to say so.

Back in her room, Rose struggled into a long nightdress that the Doctor had insisted she get. She wasn't convinced, and she decided to wear it more for novelty and authenticity than comfort. And because she was too tired even to take it off again as she collapsed into bed.

Of course, once she was in bed, Rose could not get to sleep. Every time she closed her eyes she seemed to find herself walking through yet another concrete pavilion. Her feet felt as if they had forgotten how to stop walking, and she found that she was thinking about everything in terms of exhibits. She imagined the Doctor and Wyse playing chess, and they were in front of an audience, sitting in an exhibition area on display. Each of the chess pieces seemed to be at once in the game and in a glass cabinet ready to be admired for the craftsmanship it demonstrated.

She dozed, and woke and half slept and half woke again. Everything and nothing was part of her dreams. She was walking through the club, peering into the display cabinets that seemed to be everywhere. In one of them she was startled to find Aske staring up at her. He winked. Moving on, she found Repple waiting in the next cabinet, just as she realised she had expected. But this was a working exhibit, a demonstration. The side of his face had been stripped away to reveal the workings inside – the skull and the brain. One eye stood proud, as in a diagram on the classroom wall, to show its workings, complete – impossibly – with labels.

'Why doesn't he bleed?' Freddie wanted to know. He was standing the other side of the cabinet, looking over at Rose.

'He isn't real,' she assured him. 'They're just made up for the show.'

There was a banging sound now. Like a knocking. She knew it was Aske, trying to get out of his cabinet. Knocking for help. Becoming more and more frantic. Yet she could not look away from the prone figure of Repple. 'Help him!' she shouted at Freddie.

But he shook his head. 'I might get hurt.'

Then suddenly the room went dark, and Rose realised she was awake at last. And the banging, thumping, agonised heartbeat of sound was still there above her.

Rose sat up in bed, suddenly alert as she struggled to shrug off the dream and cling to what was real. Sounds – scrapings, movement. Above her. From the ceiling, from the floor above. Then a skittering like claws, or perhaps just a suitcase being moved. Because she realised with a flush of relief that there was someone in the room above. That was all. The reclusive Mr Pooter had returned from his travels.

Even after the sounds stopped, Rose could not get back to sleep. She seemed to be more awake now than she had ever been. She was also hungry, and wished she had eaten rather more of her dinner. She lay there for a while in the near-darkness. Then she decided this was silly, and she got up and put the light on.

After a few minutes wandering round the room aimlessly, she went through to the little adjoining lounge. She waited there for several minutes, sitting on each of the chairs in turn and finding none of them comfortable. Then she went over and knocked on the connecting door to the Doctor's room. There was no answer. When she put her ear to the door, she could hear nothing. She opened the door a crack.

'Doctor? Doctor – are you awake?'

Still no answer. She held her breath, trying to listen for his breathing to tell if he was asleep. Nothing.

'Oh, this is stupid,' she said out loud. 'I can't sleep, and I don't believe you even do sleep.' She fumbled round on the wall inside the door, and found the bump of the light switch – so much more prominent than the flat white plastic light switches in her flat. It was as if someone had stuck half a cricket ball there.

The lights came on, harsh and unforgiving, to reveal a bed that was not only empty but unslept in. Typical. He was probably still playing chess. She went back to her own room to find some clothes.

* * *

'You know, sometimes I despair of the empire, I really do.' Wyse kept his fingers on the rook as he considered his move. 'Yes, why not?' he decided.

'Oh?'

'This passion for self-determination and allowing colonies to secede.'

'Not in favour?' The Doctor considered his next move. He blew out a long breath; it really was quite difficult. Wyse was a clever and skilful opponent, and the Doctor was just itching to move something and be done with it.

'All right as an ideal, I suppose. But where's it going to end? I mean, look what's happened in Ireland, and that's not over by a long chalk, I'll warrant.'

'Well, quite.' The Doctor knew where it was going to end, and he was careful to neither agree nor disagree.

'A strong central government, that's what we need. An overriding philosophy, with some local leeway.'

'You reckon?'

'Well, it's that or let them slip back to barbarity. Take the United States, fr'instance.'

'Barbarous,' the Doctor agreed with a smile.

'No, no. I mean they manage to maintain a federal system. Albeit with a rather more cohesive geography and an approximation at least of the English language.'

'Isn't that what the Commonwealth is all about?'

'Is it?' Wyse moved one of his knights forward. 'Thought that was about giving up power while trying to keep face. Recipe for disaster, in my opinion. Loss of control. Seems to me we're in danger of feeling ashamed of an empire we should be proud of. Oh, and that's check, by the way,' he pointed out.

'Maybe there are things to be ashamed of too.' Without bothering to look at the board, the Doctor moved his king out of check.

'Oh, undoubtedly,' Wyse agreed. 'Lots of 'em, I'm sure. But denying the good things doesn't make the bad ones any better, does it? Best to own up to everything, good and bad. Always a trade-off.' He removed the Doctor's queen and put his knight on the square where she had been. 'See what I mean?'

'Sure you wanted to do that?' the Doctor asked, eyes glittering in the firelight.

'What?' Wyse inspected the board, and frowned. 'Blast it.' He leaned back in his chair, pushed his monocle into his eye, and smiled. 'You know, Doctor, you should try running an empire. I've a feeling you'd be rather good at it.'

The Doctor smiled back. 'Another game?'

The moon was hidden behind smoky clouds so that the only light was from the street lamps as they struggled to cast a glow through the thin, swirling fog. The Imperial Club was locked up, the doorman gone, the lights out. Asleep for the night. Or so Cheshunt and Matty hoped as they made their way cautiously to the back of the building.

Matty was carrying a heavy bullseye lantern which he contrived to shine everywhere except where Cheshunt wanted it. It would be easier for Cheshunt to take it himself, he knew. But what was the point of being in charge if you did everything yourself?

'Seems quiet enough,' he grunted, jabbing a meaty finger at the back door in an effort to persuade Matty to hold the light over the lock. Once he could see, it was a matter of a few moments with a picklock, and they were inside.

Cheshunt had a rough sketch map of the interior. He had not asked the woman in the mask where she'd got it. He was not sure he wanted to know the answer – or what had happened to the person who had provided it. But it served to show the way through the service areas and servants' quarters at the back of the building.

They had decided to start with the foyer and the club's records. If all went according to plan, they could then move on to the Doctor's rooms. Both Cheshunt and Matty were used to searching rooms while their owners slept on in their nearby beds, oblivious. Each of them was carrying a small hessian sack which had accompanied them on many previous expeditions of a similar nature.

It all started to go wrong as they emerged into the main foyer. Cheshunt held up his hand to stop Matty in the doorway. They stared out across the marbled floor and the huge staircase that swept imposingly upwards.

'What is it?' Matty whispered.

'Voices,' Cheshunt said quietly. 'Listen.'

Right at the edge of his hearing, Cheshunt could make out the sound of people talking. Laughter. He led Matty to each of the several doorways off the foyer in turn. Eventually they found where the voices were coming from. The doorway gave into an oak-panelled corridor with paintings hanging on the walls. The two men crept slowly down the passageway, ready to turn and run at any moment. When they reached the end, Cheshunt motioned for Matty to stay put while he peered round the doorway and into the large, panelled room.

There were two men, quite a way across the room. They seemed to be playing some game on a table – draughts or dominoes or something. Between taking their turns, they talked and laughed together. They seemed well occupied, and if they had sat there until three in the morning, Cheshunt expected and hoped they were not about to move now. He gestured for Matty to retreat down the corridor, the voices fading behind them.

As he turned to follow, Cheshunt noticed the third occupant of the room. A cat. A black cat with triangular white markings on its front. The cat leaped down from the leather sofa where it had been stretched out. It stared across the room, as though it had seen Cheshunt, though he was sure it could not have done. Then it started across the room towards him. He turned and hurried after Matty.

Back in the foyer, Matty was already starting work on the small wooden desk that stood discreetly to the side of the main doors. The lights were turned down low, and Matty was holding the lantern in one hand while he worked on the lock with the other. Cheshunt hurried to join him, the cat already forgotten.

But he was soon reminded of it. Forcefully. The cat emerged from the corridor and hurled itself across the foyer, claws clicking a rapid rhythm on the stone floor like the ticking of a clock. It gave a screeching yowl of anger as it leaped at Cheshunt and Matty.

Cheshunt swore and stepped aside, hand raised in front of his face. Matty, intent on breaking the lock, had not seen the cat. He looked up, startled by the sound. The lamp swung wildly as he tried to get up a hand to protect himself. Claws slashed at his face. Shadows stretched and loomed in the lamplight. Matty was shouting to Cheshunt for help as the creature crashed into him, tearing and slashing and yowling.

The noise echoed round the foyer. Soon it was joined by running feet from the passageway. Cheshunt was pulling at the heavy bundle of fur that was clamped to Matty's face, ripping it away and hurling it to the floor. The cat landed on all four feet, turned in an instant, launched itself at Cheshunt.

The men from the panelled room were there now, running, shouting. Cheshunt considered bluffing, pretending he and Matty had every right to be there and asking for help to get the dratted animal away from them. But from the expression of boiling anger on the face of the man wearing the monocle, he knew there was no point.

For a moment they confronted each other. The cat was on the desk, hissing at Cheshunt. Matty was sobbing with pain, scratched head in hands. The two men stood facing them across the foyer. Then suddenly, bizarrely, the other man – the one in the dark leather jacket – grinned like an amused schoolboy.

'Hello,' he said brightly.

Somehow that was more frightening than the first man's anger or the cat's claws. The confidence and amusement of the man told Cheshunt in an instant that he had no chance of intimidating him, and little chance of escape.

'What's going on?' The voice came from the main stairs. 'Doctor?'

It distracted the two men, just for a second. Long enough for Cheshunt to grab Matty and push him roughly towards the main doors.

The cat hissed again, and leaped. But Cheshunt was ready for it now. He ignored the young woman running down the stairs, the two men starting across the foyer. He let the sack he was holding fall open in one hand. With the other he caught the cat in mid-air, felt its uncanny strength, somehow managed to bundle it into the sack and pull the strings at the top closed.

Matty had opened the door, bolts scraping and lock protesting. The two of them tumbled out, down the steps, and ran.

'Thanks, Rose,' came the sarcastic voice of the man from behind them. There was a clatter of feet in pursuit, rapid down the steps behind them. Cheshunt did not turn to see who was following. He ran after Matty, holding the sack at arm's length, desperate not to be scratched by the frantic, dagger-sharp claws that lashed through the heavy material. He would dump the wretched animal as soon as he got the chance. And he knew exactly where, he thought – the only pleasant thought in his mind right now.

* * *

What are you doing? Rose asked herself. There was no way she could catch the two intruders, and even if she did they were hardly going to come quietly back to the Imperial Club to apologise and explain themselves. She slowed to a jog as the two men ahead of her reached the end of the bridge.

The moon was struggling through the thin clouds and the start of a rain shower had dispelled the last wisps of fog, so she could see them clearly. The small man still had his hands over his face. The larger man was talking to him. As Rose watched, he held up the bag. She could see it moving, struggling, squirming as the cat inside struggled to be free.

In a moment, she knew what the man was going to do, and she was running again. But there was no way she could get there in time. With a loud bellow of laughter, the man let the bag drop. Then the two of them were running again.

Rose reached the bridge and looked over. She could see the murky water below reflecting back a broken image of the moon. The rain was getting heavier, peppering the surface of the river. The pale neck of the bag was just disappearing under the water, the strings hesitating a moment before following it down. Rose stared in disbelief. He'd done it, he'd really done it – chucked the poor thing into the river. She stared down, wondering if it was too late to jump in and try to find the bag. She thought of the cold, murky water, the length of the drop to the river, how she would ever get out again – or not. No bubbles broke the surface of the Thames. Rose stood there, staring down at the river, half expecting – hoping, willing – the cat to come struggling to the surface spitting water and hissing with fear. But there was nothing.

She shivered, swallowed, and turned reluctantly away.

The lights were on and the doors were open back at the Imperial Club. The unflappable Crowther was in the foyer, examining the desk that the men had been trying to open. He nodded at Rose, not at all surprised to see her come in, hair slicked down by the rain.

'There's tea in the Bastille Room, miss,' he said, as if serving tea at gone three in the morning was as natural as breathing.

'What do you think they were after?' Rose asked.

Crowther sniffed. 'Money, I expect, miss. Not that they would have found any.'

'I thought they might be after something of Mr Pooter's,' Rose said.

'Really, miss, why is that?'

She shrugged. 'I heard he was back, that's all. I thought maybe he'd brought something valuable with him.'

Crowther was shaking his head. 'I'm afraid you're mistaken. There is a trustees' meeting tomorrow, but Mr Pooter has not yet returned. I don't expect him until the meeting, late tomorrow morning. That is,' he corrected himself, 'late this morning.'

'But I heard someone in his room. Above mine. Tonight. I'm sure.'

Crowther was frowning now. 'That isn't possible, miss. Mr Pooter isn't here, and no one else would be in his rooms. I can assure you of that. Unless the intruders…'

Rose shook her head. 'No, no, before that. Ages ago.' She shrugged. 'I must be wrong,' she said, though she knew she wasn't. Something to tell the Doctor, Rose decided.

But when she arrived in the Bastille Room all thoughts of the noises from the room above were driven from her mind. The Doctor and Wyse were sitting with Aske and Repple and several other members of the club who looked as if they had dressed in haste when they heard the disturbance. Most of them were sipping tea and staring at each other through bleary eyes. Only the Doctor, Wyse and Repple seemed awake and alert. Aske was yawning.

And on the sofa beside Wyse, stretched out so he could tickle it under the chin, was a black cat. It turned as Rose approached, watching her through its emerald eyes, the triangular patch of white fur on its front catching the glow of the firelight as it purred contentedly.

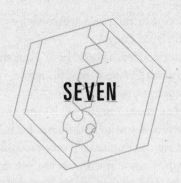

SEVEN

It was a crisp morning. The Doctor was able to blow long streams of mist from his mouth into the cold air. He took pleasure in stepping on last night's puddles, his feet breaking through the thin crust of ice and splashing into the water below. Once he misjudged it and his foot skidded on the ice without breaking the surface. He struggled to retain his balance, arms flailing like a windmill. He laughed long and loud, drawing the bemused attention of several other people hurrying through the cold of the morning.

The Doctor and Rose had sat up most of the rest of the night with Wyse before Rose finally went to catch some more sleep after a bite of breakfast and a mouthful of coffee. Wyse, like the Doctor, seemed none the worse for having been up all night.

'Often took the night watch in the trenches,' he confessed. 'The lads seemed to appreciate it.'

'You were an officer?' the Doctor asked.

'Lowly captain. Spent three years staring at mud and

bloodshed. Got to the point where you couldn't tell one from the other, you know.'

The Doctor nodded. 'I know,' he said quietly.

'You in the war?' Wyse wanted to know.

'Been in many wars. Far too many.'

'Thought as much. You can tell. It's there in the eyes. And the attitude too. A sort of enthusiasm for life between the ennui. Like we can't quite believe we're still here, but we must make the most of it while we are.' He sighed and nodded at the chess set on the table between them. 'Best stick to chess. Far less dangerous.'

'Usually,' the Doctor agreed with a smile.

Life itself was taking on some of the more intriguing aspects of a game of chess, the Doctor decided as he made his way to Sir George's. The break-in the previous night would appear to have as little to do with the loss of the TARDIS as would the advance of an outlying pawn on the fate of a king. But there was a connection, he was sure. Just as the loss and return of his coat were something more than they seemed. You had to start somewhere, and the coat was as good a place as any.

Besides, he liked a mystery.

It was a respectable hour by the time he arrived. Dickson was, as ever, courteous and unflappable. He offered to take the Doctor's coat, but the Doctor smiled and kept it. 'Not that I think it might go missing again,' he assured Dickson. 'But I want to talk to young Freddie about it. Among other things.'

'You don't think...' Dickson blurted uncharacteristically.

The Doctor raised an eyebrow and cocked his head, inviting Dickson to continue. But the man cleared his throat, embarrassed, and said nothing more.

'No, I don't,' the Doctor assured him. 'He's a good lad. I like him too. Thought he'd want to hear about the exhibition.'

Dickson's mouth twitched in the ghost of a smile, as if acknowledging that he had been found out. 'He'll be pleased to see you, Doctor. He doesn't get a lot of visitors. Shall I inform Sir George that you are visiting?'

The Doctor smiled back. 'Do. There are no secrets here.'

Dickson left the Doctor in the drawing room as he went to find Freddie.

'Unlike some places,' the Doctor went on, quietly, to himself.

Freddie was excited to see the Doctor. He asked him all about the British Empire Exhibition. The Doctor was happy to describe their visit and went through a catalogue of what they had seen, rewarded by Freddie's evident interest. The boy asked endless questions, and the Doctor patiently answered them. Sir George put his head round the door at one point, listened to the conversation for a few moments, then smiled and nodded at the Doctor, and left them to it.

After more than an hour, the Doctor finished his description. He held up his hand to curtail any more questions, and told Freddie, 'Now I've something I want to ask you.'

Freddie was sitting sideways on a sofa, with his weak leg up on a cushion. 'Anything.'

'Remember yesterday, when Rose and I came to see you, I asked you about my coat?'

Freddie nodded.

'You said "I saw her with it."'

'Yes. The Painted Lady. I saw her with your coat.'

'I didn't realise what you were telling me. I'm sorry. I know she didn't come here yesterday so you must have meant during the dinner party. You were watching from the landing, weren't you?'

Freddie nodded. He was biting his lower lip anxiously.

'You're not in trouble,' the Doctor assured him. 'You could be a hero.'

'A hero?'

The Doctor grinned. 'I'm very attached to my coat. Tell me about it.'

'I was watching, from the landing. Listening to everyone talking. I could hear voices from the dining room when the door was open. That was when I heard...' He paused, looked away. 'Then everyone was leaving. Rose saw me watching. I thought she would give me away, tell Father.'

'Rose wouldn't do that,' the Doctor said gently.

'I know. But I was still worried. Then, after Rose went, the lady in the mask was left alone. And she went back into the dining room. I was going to go back to bed, but I wanted to know what she was doing. She said she was leaving, then she stayed.'

'Curious?'

'Yes. She's mysterious. She needs investigating.'

'You investigate lots of people?'

'Loads. I have a notebook, I write down everything about them.'

The Doctor smiled. 'Really? What've you written about me?'

Freddie grinned. 'She wasn't gone long, the Painted Lady. She had your coat. I like your coat. It looks so comfortable and warm and… right.'

'What did she do then?'

'She went.'

'Taking my coat. Just like that?'

Freddie nodded. 'She felt in the pockets first. She found something she was interested in. A silver rod or something.'

'This?' He held up the sonic screwdriver for Freddie to see.

'Yes, that's it. She looked at it. She seemed interested.'

'I bet.'

'Then she heard someone coming. Dickson with the port, I think. She left quickly. And I went back to bed.' He hesitated, then asked, 'Does that help? Is that what you wanted to hear?'

The Doctor clicked his tongue. 'Yes and no,' he decided. 'It helps. It isn't what I wanted to hear.' He stood up and pulled his coat tight about him as if checking it still fitted. 'See you then,' he told Freddie. A thought occurred to him as he made to leave. The Doctor turned back, not surprised to find Freddie watching him attentively.

'Do you want to try the coat on?' the Doctor asked. He could see the answer at once from the boy's expression, and he slipped off the jacket and held it out.

It was miles too big of course. But Freddie pulled back the sleeves and grinned. 'Can I keep it?'

The Doctor laughed. 'Afraid not. I'd get cold.' He waited

for Freddie to hand back the coat. As he took it, while Freddie was still holding it, the Doctor looked into Freddie's eyes. 'Look after yourself,' he said, quietly. 'Leave me to investigate Melissa Heart, all right?'

The boy let go of the coat, and turned away. 'All right.'

It didn't surprise Rose that the Doctor had wandered off somewhere without leaving her a note or a message. Crowther was able to tell her simply that he had gone out early that morning.

The head steward seemed preoccupied, and Rose recalled that he had told her there was a trustees' meeting late that morning and Mr Pooter was expected. That in turn reminded her of the noises she had heard from the room above the night before. Could it have been the intruders? Had they been on the top floor, perhaps even come in that way? There was no way of knowing, of course, unless the reclusive Mr Pooter returned to discover his rooms had been disturbed.

She looked for Wyse to see if he knew where the Doctor had gone, or when he might be back. But there was no sign of him in the Bastille Room. Aske and Repple were talking quietly in a corner. She could hear Repple's righteous tones as he described how unjustly he had been deposed. Aske was doing his best to sympathise. They looked up as Rose approached, and both seemed relieved to see that it was her. But neither of them knew where the Doctor was.

'Wyse may be out visiting,' Aske suggested. 'He plays chess against a friend every Wednesday.'

'Is it Wednesday?' Rose asked. 'I lose track.'

'He usually goes in the evening, though,' Repple pointed out. 'He could be anywhere. Sorry.'

The only useful information they were able to impart was that the trustees' meeting was likely to take place in what they called the boardroom on the first floor. And because she had nothing better to do, Rose decided she might as well see if she could find where this was. She might also get a glimpse of the elusive Mr Pooter, she thought with a smile.

It was immediately apparent which was the boardroom. There was a uniformed club steward standing outside, though whether on guard or waiting to attend to any orders for tea and biscuits it was impossible to tell. It did mean, though, that Rose wouldn't be listening at the door.

Which was a shame, she thought. She was quite intrigued to see the mysterious Mr Pooter and there was the added incentive that they might well be talking about the circumstances of herself and the Doctor. Wyse had suggested he would sponsor their application to stay at the club, and with the Doctor showing no apparent signs of even looking for the TARDIS, having somewhere to stay seemed like a pretty good move.

It had struck Rose that as much of the difference of London in the 1920s was to do with what was missing as what was changed. True, the cars and clothes and buildings were different. But there was no London Eye dominating the low-rise skyline. There was no loud music in the streets, little traffic noise, practically no planes. No road markings or personal stereos or T-shirt slogans. And inside the building she had realised that there were no fire-exit signs or smoke detectors.

But there was a fire escape. A galvanised metal gantry on each floor at the back of the building, with precarious-looking metal steps to each level on the lower floors that became a distinctly treacherous-looking ladder as it reached more than halfway up the building. The gantry on the first floor was reached not from a fire door, but by climbing out of a window of one of the larger rooms – the boardroom. Which meant, Rose reasoned, that if she got on to the fire escape from the floor above, she could sneak down and perhaps get a look at the trustees through the window. Was it worth the effort, she wondered? What the heck, she'd nothing else to do.

Halfway down, she was not sure this was a terrific idea. The stairway creaked and cracked under her weight. Was it her imagination, or was the whole thing swaying as she moved? How was it fixed to the building anyway – surely it couldn't be just that bolt sticking out of the crumbling stonework? But it was as far to go back now as it was to creep down to the metal balcony and edge along until she could see into the boardroom. If only the late morning sun hadn't been shining directly at the glass, she could have seen in from higher up, from where she was.

She crept as close as she dared, leaning out so that the sunlight no longer glinted back in her eyes. Sure enough, she could see into the room from here. But it was rather a restricted view. The window was shut, so she could hear nothing. If she went any closer she might have a better view and might even catch a few words, but she then risked being seen. So she crouched down where she was and stared, disappointed, at the shoulders-to-waist view she had of several men in suits. The top of the table was clearly visible, with its array of papers, pens, notes, and resting hands. One of the hands drummed bored fingers on the polished surface. Another was bunched into a fist and crashed down to emphasise whatever point the speaker was making.

The chair at the head of the table was pushed back. There were no papers or notes in front of the man sitting there, and because of how the chair was angled, Rose could see all of the man from the neck down. Immaculate pinstriped suit, dark socks and polished shoes. Mr Pooter, she presumed. Sitting incongruously in the man's lap was the cat. She could clearly see the distinctive white triangle of fur, and she couldn't help smiling at how the creature must have escaped from the river.

Pooter was holding the cat with one hand, almost protectively. His other hand was bunched into a fist, and he rubbed his knuckles into the cat's head. The cat seemed unperturbed, and Rose could imagine it purring at the attention. Its ears stood upright and alert, its green eyes flicking back and forth as if it was listening to every word of the meeting.

Realising she was going to learn nothing of interest, Rose took a careful, crouched step backwards, towards the steps up to the second floor. But not careful enough. Her foot scraped along the metal gantry, and the whole fire escape creaked ominously. She froze.

Inside the room there was no noticeable reaction. Except

from the cat. It had turned, Pooter's knuckles still ruffling the fur on its head. Now it was staring at the window. Its emerald lozenge eyes fixed on Rose's, just for an instant. Just long enough for her to know for certain that it had seen her. Then the cat turned away, dismissing her as inconsequential. Feeling stupid, disappointed and unsettled, Rose padded away.

The Doctor was waiting for Rose in the foyer. He gave every impression of having been there for hours. He was peering with interest at a painting, tapping one foot impatiently. Rose guessed he had just nipped in ahead of her and that it was all an act. But she couldn't be sure.

'There you are,' he said without looking as she crept up behind him.

'Yeah. Where have you been?'

'Saw Freddie.' Now the Doctor did turn. He grinned at her like a schoolboy. 'Thought I'd check to be sure before venturing into the lion's den. Lioness's den,' he corrected himself.

'Check what?'

Without really noticing, she had followed him out of the club and into the street. The Doctor licked his finger and held it in the air for a moment as he decided which way to go. 'That Melissa Heart took my coat. Deliberately.'

'She's the lioness?'

'Let's find out.'

'How do we do that then?' She had to hurry to keep up.

The Doctor was striding off at speed, with a sudden sense of purpose. 'We go and ask her. Keep up.'

'That'll surprise her.'

'Doubt it.' He paused to get his bearings at a junction, then hurried across the road, waving absently at a horse that drew up sharply to avoid hitting them. 'She made a point of telling us where she lives. Twice.'

'Invitation?'

'Yep.'

'She's expecting us?'

'Probably wondering what's taking us so long. Probably thinks we're being a bit thick.'

'Whereas in fact…' Rose muttered.

'I like people to think I'm a bit thick,' the Doctor declared, to the amusement of a passing couple. 'Makes them careless and arrogant. Ready to explain their dastardly plan in words of one sill… silly…' He struggled to get his mouth round the word.

'Syllable?'

'That's it.'

'I got English,' Rose told him.

'Then tell me…' He stopped abruptly and turned to her, eyes dark and serious.

'Yes?'

'I've always wondered, why isn't phonetic spelled with an "F"?'

Rose stared back at him. 'I can teach you how to spell Doctor with an "F".'

They carried on walking. After a while, Rose said, 'I saw Mr Pooter this morning.'

'Oh? What's he look like?'

'Dunno. Only saw him from the neck down. Smart,

I s'pose. Dapper. Suit. You know. Likes cats.'

'Doesn't mean he's a bad person.'

The Doctor stopped, looking up and down the street. They were beside the Thames. Rose could smell the river.

'Yes,' the Doctor decided, and walked up the path to the nearest house. 'Here we are.' The bell pull was a long metal rod hanging down beside the front door. The Doctor gave it a tug, and somewhere deep inside the house they could hear the bell jangling.

The door opened almost at once. Melissa Heart was standing there, her face a Pierrot split of black and white. A single white teardrop broke the varnished black of the left side of the mask. 'Why, Doctor, and Rose, this is unexpected,' she said without a hint of surprise. 'You do keep turning up. Like a bad wolf.'

'Penny,' Rose corrected her.

The Doctor grinned. 'Actually she's Rose. The phrase is, "like a bad penny".' His grin faded. 'Have trouble with the local idioms, do you?'

'I know an idiom when I see one,' Melissa said coolly. 'Tell me, are you here to put a smile on my face? Do come in, let me offer you a cup of tea.'

The Doctor sniffed. 'So, too late for lunch then?'

Across the street a lone figure stood in the shadow of a tree. It watched the door open, saw Melissa Heart standing there. It looked on with interest as she stepped aside to allow the Doctor and Rose to enter the house.

A cab rattled past, obscuring the view of the house for

several moments. When it had passed, the door was closed and the Doctor and Rose had gone. The figure stood watching, thinking…

The house was deep, running back to the river. Rose could see the boats on the Thames from the window of the large room that Melissa took them to. But it was not the view that caught her attention.

Melissa Heart led them to a group of armchairs arranged around a low table. On the table was a teapot, sugar bowl and milk jug and three cups.

'I hope you've not made the tea too many times while you waited,' the Doctor said. 'We had other appointments.'

She poured the tea without comment.

'Deceptively spacious,' the Doctor went on, hands in pockets as he looked round. 'Doesn't look so big from outside. Which reminds me,' he went on, slumping down into one of the chairs, 'We've mislaid some property. You don't know where it is, I suppose?'

The mask stared at him blankly.

'Thought not.' He raised the teacup, as if in a toast, then pointedly put it back on the saucer without drinking.

The room was large, but dominated by a long table that ran down one side of it. At the far end of the room, windows gave out on to a short terrace beside the river. On the left wall was a large fireplace, and in alcoves either side of it two matching suits of armour stood on low plinths. Their faces were blank polished metal visors. Each rested its clenched metal gauntlets on the pommel of a long sword that jabbed into the plinth between its feet.

The wall opposite the fireplace was adorned with several oil paintings and a large shield with two more swords crossed behind it. The wallpaper had faded and the paint-work was peeling. Dust lay everywhere, as if Melissa Heart had taken up temporary residence in an empty, abandoned house and made only the barest attempt to settle in.

Rose had not sat down. She was standing beside the long, polished wooden table that ran the length of the room. Arranged along it was a line of masks. There must be twenty or more, she thought. She recognised the ornate butterfly mask that Melissa had worn when they first met at Sir George's.

There were others that were just as stylised. Some had crude expressions painted on them with bold, iconic strokes. A broad uplifting smile contrasted with its neighbour – a mouth drooping with sadness and tears dripping from the eyes. Further along, a face with straight mouth, wrinkled forehead and crow's feet round the dark-rimmed eyes stared angrily at the ceiling. One white face was completely blank…

'Why do you wear masks all the time?' Rose asked. After all, why not be direct?

Melissa picked up the happy face. She turned away from them briefly, and when she turned back she was smiling. She put the Pierrot mask in the space where the smile had been.

'Some say it is because I am so beautiful none can look at me. Others say it is because I am so ugly.'

'Beauty's in the eye of the beholder,' the Doctor said. 'So it's possible both those theories are true.' He leaped to his feet and surveyed the masks arranged on the table. 'A face for every occasion.'

'You think I am beautiful?' Melissa asked. She sounded amused.

'Beauty's only mask deep. Maybe you just don't like people to see your face.'

'Why?' Rose asked. 'Zits?'

'Could be,' the Doctor agreed. 'Or she's afraid her face will give away what she's really thinking. How much better to wear a mask to show others what she'd like them to see.'

'Isn't that what everyone does?' Melissa asked. 'Perhaps I am simply more honest about it.' She turned, the mask pointing straight at the Doctor. 'How honest are you, Doctor? Are you really what you seem to be?'

The Doctor's face twitched into a half-smile. 'And what do I seem to be?'

'A man out of his time and place, judging by what you keep in your pockets. By the way your jacket is made and the company you keep.'

'Oi, don't be rude,' Rose said.

Melissa did not turn, but her voice was steel-edged. 'Please don't make me wear my angry face. Your manner, your demeanour, your vocabulary, your attitude. They all mark you out as an exception here.'

'And you're interested in exceptions?'

'Only one. Are you the one I'm searching for, Doctor? I rather think you are.'

'I rather think I don't know what you're talking about.'

Now Melissa did turn to Rose. 'You shield him, protect

him despite everything, don't you? Adhering to the letter of the law. Despite what he has done.'

'What has he done?'

'Yes,' the Doctor said brightly, 'do tell.'

'Don't be crass!' In a single gesture Melissa scooped up the angry mask from the table and held it in front of her smiling face. The smile slid out from behind and the angry face was pushed into place in its stead. 'I warned you not to anger me. You know what I am talking about. Why I am here.'

'Humour us,' the Doctor said. 'Why are you here?'

Her voice was disconcertingly level and controlled behind the angry mask. 'Why, to kill you of course.'

She stepped back and snapped her fingers – a gunshot of sound in the large room. As the noise faded, Rose became aware of another sound – a background ticking. Instinctively, she glanced at the empty mantel above the large fireplace across the room.

So she was looking almost straight at one of the suits of armour when it shuddered and moved. It lifted the heavy sword in its metal hands and stepped stiffly down from the low plinth. The featureless mask of its helmet swung slowly, jerkily at first, as it scanned the room. It paused, seeming to see Melissa Heart. Then it fixed on the Doctor as he stepped across and took Rose's hand. He was tense, ready to run.

The suit of armour stared blankly at the Doctor and Rose. The sword raised slowly, poised to strike the killing blow as it lumbered towards them, cutting off their escape. Its internal mechanisms and gears were clicking through their inexorable motions like the ticking of a clock.

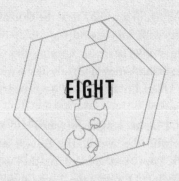

EIGHT

'Clockwork, I assume,' the Doctor said. 'How clever.' He sounded calm, but his eyes were moving rapidly as he hunted for a way of escape.

'More clever than you have been,' the Painted Lady told him. She had stepped away from the Doctor and Rose to allow the clockwork automaton to approach them. Its sword was still poised, ready to strike.

'Oh?'

'I know how important it is to use one's initiative and avoid traceable, anachronistic technology.'

'Ah.'

'That was how I found you, of course.'

'Of course. The TARDIS, and then the sonic screwdriver,' he explained to Rose.

'I almost dismissed the readings at first, they were so far off the scale. And just when I was thinking you were not on this little planet at all. That all my efforts would be for nothing.'

'Been looking for a while then,' the Doctor said. He was pulling Rose with him round the table, away from the approaching suit of armour, keeping the table between them. Melissa's mask moved slightly as she watched.

'Faceless killers on the streets,' Rose said. 'Wonder who that could be then.'

The metal figure lunged forwards suddenly, slashing downwards with the sword. The Doctor and Rose both jumped back. The sword whistled past the Doctor and sliced into the table. It cut through the Pierrot mask, neatly dividing black from white. The Doctor reached across and grabbed at the blade, trying to pull it away from the knight.

His hand came away cut and bloodied. 'Maybe not,' he said. 'That's sharp.'

'More than she is,' Rose retorted. 'Who's she really looking for?'

The Doctor shrugged. 'Someone you expected to meet at Sir George's, was it? You already had your suspicions. Some alien cuckoo in the nest of 1920s London? You can't have been sure, because you still came to see me.'

Melissa Heart did not reply. Her face stared at them as blankly as the clockwork knight's.

Rose was thinking about what the Doctor had said. The implications. 'She's alien?'

'Behind the mask.' He glanced towards the door, checking the way was clear. 'Well, must dash. Sorry.'

But as they turned to run, the second of the two knights beside the fireplace jerked into mechanical life and stepped swiftly across to block the way.

'So much for initiative,' Rose said.

'Diplomacy?' the Doctor wondered. 'Don't suppose you'd care to discuss the mistake you're making?'

Melissa stepped up beside the table, tapping an elegant finger next to the happy mask. 'Don't make me laugh.'

The Doctor sighed. 'Thought not. Anachronistic technology it is then.' He pulled the sonic screwdriver out of his pocket, aimed it squarely at the clockwork knight now approaching them from the doorway, and…

Nothing happened.

Melissa was wearing the smiling happy mask now. 'I did of course remove the power source before I returned that device to you.'

They were trapped between the two advancing knights. Swords were raised, poised, ready to strike down at them.

'Don't s'pose you have a mask showing smug self-satisfaction, do you?' the Doctor wondered.

'It would suit her,' Rose agreed. She swallowed, her throat dry. Then she saw where the Doctor was looking – over Melissa's shoulder and out towards the Thames. Saw the figure standing at the window, desperately pushing at it from the outside.

'Not for her,' the Doctor was saying. 'If you had smug self-satisfaction, you see…' He paused, as Freddie finally managed to heave the window open. 'I'd like to borrow it! Come on, Rose.'

The swords crashed down, splitting the air where the Doctor and Rose had been a second before. Together, they leaped up on to the table, and jumped off across the room past Melissa Heart. Ran towards the open window. Behind them the knights' ticking did not miss a beat as they both turned and started round the table, following the Doctor and Rose.

'Thanks, Freddie,' Rose gasped as she hurled herself after the Doctor through the window.

'Don't hang about,' the Doctor called back.

Rose grabbed Freddie's hand, and they ran stumbling after the Doctor.

There was an alleyway leading round to the front of the houses, and they slowed to a walk once they were back on the road. Even so, Freddie struggled to keep up. He seemed both confused and euphoric.

'What were those things? People in armour? Why were they attacking you? I didn't get hurt. Not at all.' He inspected his hands closely as they walked, making Rose smile. 'I was afraid I'd cut myself opening the window. There were splinters and everything.'

'Can be nasty, splinters,' the Doctor agreed.

'Better not tell your mum,' Rose added. 'She'd go spare.'

Freddie nodded. 'She'd be upset and worried.'

'She'll be worried if you don't hurry home,' the Doctor pointed out. 'I'd come with you, but…'

'We're being followed?' Rose said, looking round.

'Probably. There again, she has the TARDIS and she knows that's important. I'll be back, to coin a phrase.'

'And those knights are really clockwork men?'

Freddie's eyes widened. 'Clockwork?'

'Yeah. We're not winding you up,' Rose said.

The Doctor grinned at her, then turned quickly away. 'Of a kind, Freddie. Self-winding, I imagine. The movement is self-perpetuating, at least to a point. They never stop. They never give up.'

'And they're after us. Great.'

'Nice to be wanted. Wish I knew why.'

'The Painted Lady wants to kill you?' Freddie said.

'Oh yes,' the Doctor realised. 'That's why.' He frowned. 'Nope.'

'Nope?' Rose checked.

'Nope,' he assured her. 'That doesn't help. She's looking for someone she wants to kill. Isn't even sure they're...' He paused, glancing at Freddie. 'In London. Then she finds us and she's convinced, wrongly, that it's me she wants.'

'But she was off to Freddie's stepdad's anyway,' Rose said.

'She's very thorough,' the Doctor decided. 'So either the target isn't here, or else they're very thorough too. Very clever. Very good at it.'

'At what?'

'At hiding.'

'Which means, they know she's looking,' Rose realised.

'They know someone is.'

'We're going back to the club,' the Doctor said to Freddie. 'I really do think you should get home. OK?'

Freddie nodded solemnly. 'All right, Doctor. But you will tell me what happens? If I can help?'

The Doctor reached out suddenly and shook his hand. 'You've already helped. You've saved our lives.' He nodded in appreciation. 'You're a hero.'

Freddie grinned. The grin froze, then faded as Rose leaned over and kissed him on the cheek. 'Thanks,' she said.

He was rubbing the cheek as he walked away, glancing round embarrassed.

'I only kissed him,' Rose said.

'He's a boy,' the Doctor told her.

'I thought that's what they were for,' she grumbled, following him down the street.

'Right, the plan,' the Doctor announced as they reached the Imperial Club.

'Ready,' Rose affirmed.

'Melissa will send her clockwork cronies after us as soon as it's dark.'

'Sure?'

He nodded. 'She's impatient now she thinks she's found me. And she's thrown caution to the wind. So we need to warn the other guests and organise some defences.'

'Or run away?'

'Putting off the inevitable. Here we know the territory, and we have friends. Anyway, she'll trash the place looking for us whether we're here or not.'

'So where do we start?'

The Doctor tapped his chin as he thought. 'You've seen Mr Pooter, so you go and convince him of the danger. I'll find Wyse and the others.'

'I haven't seen Mr Pooter,' Rose protested. 'Well, I mean I have seen him. But I haven't seen him.' She paused, a

thought coalescing in her mind. 'Hang on. Reclusive charac-
ter, hiding away, no one ever sees him… You don't think…?'

'No. He'd hardly hide away from assassins by adopting a
laughably silly name then opening a club in central London
and taking in guests.'

'No?'

'No. That's the daft sort of double-bluff I'd do to draw out
the enemy. Dangerous and ill-advised. Go on. Then meet me
in the Bastille Room sharpish.'

'Yes, sir!' Rose snapped an ironic salute and started up the
stairs.

The Doctor turned to find Crowther watching him.
'You'd better come and listen to this too,' the Doctor told
him. 'How many guests are staying here at the moment?'

'Besides yourselves, Doctor, and Wyse…' Crowther
counted on his fingers as he followed the Doctor along the
panelled corridor. 'There's old Sir Henry, but he's confined
to bed. Oliver Maffeking has gone to stay with friends
tonight. Now that the Hansons have moved on, that just
leaves Ranskill, Coleridge, Wensleydale. Several others. And
Repple and Aske, of course.'

'And the staff.'

'Indeed, sir.'

Wyse was sitting in his usual chair. He looked up as the
Doctor entered, and smiled and nodded in greeting.

'Find Aske and Repple and the other guests and see if they
can join us,' the Doctor said to Crowther. 'And any of the
staff who are about.'

'Is it important, Doctor?'

'Vital. Go on.'

The Doctor walked slowly over to join Wyse. 'I've a story to tell you,' he said. 'A true story, though you might find it hard to believe.'

'How intriguing.' The man's eyes glinted with amusement and he gestured for the Doctor to sit down. 'I've heard some pretty rum stories in me time, I can tell you. So, what's this one all about then, eh?'

'It's about a Painted Lady. It's about clockwork killers. A manhunt. Mistaken identity. Assassination. The usual ingredients.'

'Might be usual for you, Doctor,' Wyse said. His eyes met the Doctor's deep gaze. 'Yes, might very well be. You know,' he said, standing up, 'I was thinking it was a tad early for a brandy just now. But actually I think I will. Join me?'

'If it makes you feel better.'

Several decanters were arranged on a low table by the fireplace. Wyse poured two brandies, then returned to his chair, handing the Doctor one of the glasses. 'Now then,' he said. 'Shall we begin?'

The stairs ended on a small landing outside a heavy wooden door. Rose had been worried she might not be able to find Mr Pooter's rooms. But there was just the one door, no choice. No problem. Rose took a deep breath, swallowed and knocked loudly on the door.

There was no answer. She knocked again. Still nothing, so she pressed her ear to the door. There were sounds coming from inside, she was sure. Movement, a hum like a fridge. Ticking of a clock.

Rose stepped back from the door, suddenly unnerved. What if it wasn't a clock? What if…?

Then the door opened. Or rather, a part of the door opened. It was heavy, dark wood, made of several rectangular panels separated by beading. One of the panels at the bottom of the door swung open. Light spilled out on to the bare boards of the landing. Harsh, white light.

She stepped back. trying to see through the open panel. But she could make out nothing but the light. Then slowly a shape formed within it. Something was coming out. Something dark, silhouetted against the artificial light.

With a laugh of relief, Rose realised it was the cat. It stepped out on to the landing, claws clicking rhythmically on the wooden floor. She reached out to stroke it, but her hand froze in mid-air.

The white triangle of fur under the cat's head was stark against the black body as the creature looked up at Rose. Its lozenge-shaped emerald eyes fixed on her. And suddenly they were no longer green, but red. Deep, blood red as if lit from within.

The animal's mouth opened wide in a hiss of anger. Surprised, Rose straightened up and took a step backwards. Her foot slipped over the top step and she lurched sideways with a cry – arm out to grab the banister rail and save herself from falling. At the same moment as she almost fell, the eyes blazed. Two beams of electric red shot out from the cat's eyes, scorching their way across the wall behind where Rose had been.

The cat's head snapped round as it reacquired its target. Rose pressed herself back against the wall, ducking as the rays scythed out again. Smoke drifted from the scarred wall. Rose shrieked, throwing her hands up in front of her face as the cat leaped. Claws out, it hurled itself at Rose, eyes blazing with lethal fury.

NINE

There was silence when the Doctor finished his story. He had not told them everything, of course. Just enough. Start spouting nonsense about being an alien from the future and he might lose them altogether. So he stuck to the bare bones of the story – mysterious clockwork killers sent by a masked woman to assassinate the wrong man. Straightforward enough.

The staff who had gathered with Crowther to listen to the latter part of the Doctor's story exchanged looks – some worried, some amused, some just confused. Several guests were sitting close by, listening attentively. Aske and Repple were the only ones the Doctor knew by name. Repple in particular was watching the Doctor closely, his face set expressionless. Aske looked from the Doctor to Repple and back again – was he wondering how this would affect his patient's mind, or somehow assimilating it into his own delusions?

Wyse held up his glass and swirled round the last drops

of the pale liquid in the bottom of the bowl. He finished the drink and stood up. 'Glad I had that brandy,' he said. 'Think I might have another. Anyone else?' He raised his eyebrows enquiringly at the Doctor, then turned to include the staff in his invitation. 'No? Then please don't mind me.'

Aske joined him at the decanters and allowed Wyse to pour generous measures into two glasses. He took one back to Repple.

Crowther cleared his throat. 'Excuse me, Doctor, but what are you suggesting we do? If I have understood correctly, you believe these assassins will be making their way here as soon as it is dark.'

'Guess so,' the Doctor agreed. 'So we all have to make our choices.' He counted them off on his fingers. 'Stand and fight. Barricade the doors and try to scare them off. Hide under the tables.' He still had a finger left and clicked his tongue as if trying to remember the final option. 'Run away,' he decided at last. 'Let them rampage about and cause trouble on their own. Maybe try to lead them off, but I doubt it'd work.'

'I shall not run away,' Repple announced. 'I think we all know who these assassins are really after.' He stood up, brandy in one hand, the other in his jacket pocket. Aske stood beside him, mirroring the stance. 'I have always known that this time might come,' Repple went on. 'That the evil forces that oppose me at home would hunt me down.'

'We can't be certain it's for your benefit,' the Doctor pointed out gently.

Repple ignored him. 'Who will stand with me in my hour of need? Which of you has the courage and the honour to do battle with the forces ranged against us?' He lifted the glass. 'To victory,' he declared. 'And to Dastaria.' Repple and Aske drank, then sat down again.

Wyse took a half-hearted sip at his brandy. 'Yes, well, be that as it may,' he said, 'I'm afraid it's Wednesday, so I don't think I shall be able to help. Prior engagement, you know. But,' he added, 'I shall hurry back in the event I can be of any assistance.'

The Doctor stared at him. 'Prior engagement?'

Wyse looked slightly embarrassed. 'Long-standing. Couldn't possibly miss it. Every Wednesday.' He pulled out a watch on a chain from his waistcoat pocket, pushed his monocle into place, and checked the time. 'Got an hour or so before I have to leave, if that's any help. But every Wednesday I play chess with a friend just along the Embankment. Never miss. Sorry. Be right back,' he added with an apologetic smile. 'But, you know – can't let the blighters win, can we? Can't let them set the rules and dictate to us how we spend our own time.'

This last comment seemed to strike a chord with Repple, who nodded grimly in agreement.

While Wyse had been talking, several staff and a few guests had taken the chance to slip away. The room was looking rather empty now. The Doctor counted off the people left – Aske and Repple, Crowther and two of his men. The remaining guests were two elderly men – one of whom the Doctor was sure was so deaf he didn't know what was being discussed – and a middle-aged gentleman of enormous girth who was grinning with eager anticipation.

The Doctor sighed. Not exactly an army, but he could not expect people to put themselves at risk for him. Or even on the off-chance that the clockwork killers might come for him. He was most saddened by Wyse, but he assumed the man had simply not believed him. Typically, he was too polite to say so outright, but equally he wasn't willing to give up his precious evening just to humour the Doctor. Understandable, but sad.

'I've sent the ladies away, Doctor,' Crowther confessed. 'I hope that was correct.'

The Doctor nodded. 'S'pose so. Too late now if it wasn't. Though Rose is always useful in a –' He broke off, looking round. 'Where is Rose?' he wondered aloud.

More from instinct than design, Rose grabbed the creature in mid-air, catching it round the neck with both hands, twisting it away so that the deadly rays traced twin black scorches across the wall behind her.

She could feel the thing writhing as she struggled to hold on. Its body was like a bag of bones – hard and brittle under the fur. It hissed and fought. Claws raked at Rose as she tried to keep it at arm's length. She knew she would not be able to hold on to it for long.

So she turned sideways, still holding the cat firmly round the neck, squeezing as tightly as she could but with no apparent effect. The beams were lancing out, gouging through the paint and panelling as the head snapped angrily round in an effort to get at Rose. Any illusion she'd had that it was a real cat, made of flesh and blood, was long gone. Rose braced her feet on the stairs, and slammed the thing's head as hard as she could into the wall.

There was an unpleasant crunching sound, and the cat gave an unearthly wail. She smashed it into the wall again, which crumbled under the impact. And again – a starburst of flaking plaster and paint. One of the eyes was still firing, blackening the wall as Rose once more swung her arms.

The light in the eye went out. But the claws were still raking, the mouth hissing in the middle of the battered face. Rose let go of the neck with one hand, grabbed the cat's tail instead. She braced herself again, let go with the other hand. Both hands now holding the cat's tail, she swung it with all her might at the wall.

With a wrenching, tearing noise like a car stripping its gears, the cat went limp in her hands. She swung it again, to be sure, to work off the adrenalin, because she didn't yet dare to believe that the thing was dead.

The cat's fur split open, as if badly stitched. Cogwheels, gears, levers, small shapes of metal tumbled from inside and clattered to the floor. They bounced down the stairs and spun across the floorboards. Rose dropped what was left of the cat. She picked her way through the scattering of brass and steel components that littered the stairs. As soon as she could, she ran.

On the landing, all was silent. Then the panel of the door to Mr Pooter's rooms opened once more. A cat stepped through, surveying the scene in front of it through emerald eyes. It was a black cat, with a white triangle of fur under its head. It paused, head cocked to one side as if listening.

Then the panel of the door swung shut, and the cat ran down the stairs. After Rose.

Even from outside it was apparent that something was happening at the Imperial Club. The figure watching from the deepening shadows, as the late afternoon turned to evening, observed with interest.

Shutters were closed over windows. The front door was closed and locked. Freddie could hear the rasp of metal on metal as the bolts were slid across. He sat down on the pavement, careful to make sure that there was nothing sharp or rough, and watched with interest. He saw the Doctor shadowed against windows before shutters swung across. He saw Rose looking out from an upstairs room and scanning the street. Freddie shuffled carefully back into the darkness, hoping she could not see him.

He wondered what would happen if the Doctor or Rose did see him. Would they ask him to come inside, away from the danger, from the clockwork knights they were obviously expecting? Or would they pack him off back home? Probably they would telephone his stepfather to come and get him, he thought. Best not to be seen. Best to watch and wait and help when and if he could.

It was getting cold now, and Freddie pulled his coat about him and hummed to himself for the company. It was a tune his father had taught him. They had whistled it together as they trudged through the snow that last night, before they sheltered in the barn. A lilting, melancholy tune. If there were words to it, he did not know them. But he could feel the emotion and the sadness that went with it. He wiped his eyes with the back of his hand, and imagined his father standing behind him as he kept watch.

The fat man was called Wensleydale. Like the cheese, as the Doctor pointed out with amusement. He had been a lieutenant in the Fusiliers, he told the Doctor and Rose. 'In younger days,' he added, patting his enormous stomach.

'Thank you for staying,' Rose said.

He laughed it off. 'Couldn't let you down. Anyway, got nothing much better to do, and can't leave decent people in the lurch.'

'Unlike Wyse,' Rose said. She turned to the Doctor. 'How could he just leave like that?'

The Doctor shrugged. 'He said he'd be back.'

'Yeah, like Schwarzenegger.'

'He did come back,' the Doctor pointed out. 'Maybe Wyse will return to save the day.'

'He's a good sort really,' Wensleydale assured them. 'But Wednesday's his chess night. Everyone knows that. Plays against some fellah named Ben something or other. Dunno where he lives, but Wyse once told me you can see his place from the Embankment. Seemed to find that amusing, but he's a cheerful cove any old how.'

'What about the cat?' Rose asked the Doctor once Wensleydale had left them.

'Dead duck.'

'No, cat. But it's dead all right. If clockwork animals can die.'

'We'll worry about it later then.'

'Think it's something to do with Melissa Heart and her clockwork knights?'

The Doctor pursed his lips and stared at her.

'OK, so big coincidence if it isn't, right?'

'Right.'

'And you really think she'll come after us?' He kept the same expression, so Rose sighed and went on, 'OK, another stupid question. Just forget I'm here, like usual.'

'Oh.' He was mortified. 'I never forget you. How could I ever forget you, Rose Taylor?'

'Tyler,' she corrected him. But they were both smiling now.

The back door of the club closed with a satisfying clunk. Almost as satisfying as the click of the key turning in the lock. Wyse slipped the key into his pocket. It was a shame to have to leave and miss all the fun, assuming there really was fun to be had, he thought.

He knew the Doctor well enough, trusted him enough, to believe that the Doctor thought the threat he described was very real. But it was, Wyse decided, a question of priority. He turned away from the door, not at all surprised to see that the cat had slipped out with him. Its eyes glowed green in the near-darkness.

Wyse crouched down and tickled the cat under the chin.

Its eyes narrowed, but it did not object. 'Right, time to be going.' Wyse straightened up and raised a hand in a farewell wave to the back of the Imperial Club.

He hummed tunelessly to himself as he emerged into the street. It looked as if it was going to be a fine evening, he thought. A bit cloudy, maybe a shower later. The inevitable London mist and fog. But generally fine. He swung his monocle happily on its chain as he strode off towards the Embankment, apparently without a care in the world.

Behind him, the cat followed along the pavement. Its eyes never left the figure ahead. When Wyse paused to listen to the hour strike, so did the cat. When he moved on, the cat kept with him. He didn't look back. He paused to nod a greeting to the two figures that passed him on the other side of the pavement, and the cat paused too.

But it did not spare the figures a glance. It did not seem to notice that they were walking stiffly and mechanically, any more than Wyse did. It did not care that they looked more like suits of medieval armour than human beings. It did not wonder at the rhythmic ticking that accompanied the two dark figures making their way towards the Imperial Club.

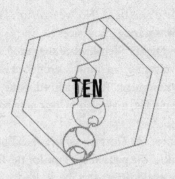

TEN

The first sign was a hammering on the front door. Quiet at first – knocking to be allowed in – the sound quickly grew to a battering. The Doctor had left one of the shutters on the first floor half open. The window gave a good view of the main door, and Rose ran to look.

'It's them,' she confirmed.

'Just two of them?' the Doctor called up the stairs from the foyer. His voice seemed to carry easily though Rose had to shout to be heard.

'Yes.'

'Melissa not with them?'

'Seems not.'

'She won't be far away.'

Rose ran back down to join the group gathered in the foyer. 'So, what now? Should we just, maybe, you know, go with them?'

'If I thought it would end there,' the Doctor said quietly. 'But it isn't really us she's after. And when she works that out…' He shook his head. 'No, we have to…' His voice tailed off, and he was staring into space.

'Stand and fight?' Wensleydale suggested. He brandished a service revolver he had proudly produced earlier.

'A noble sentiment,' Repple agreed. Aske, hand as usual in his jacket pocket, making him look nonchalant and aloof, said nothing.

'On balance,' the Doctor said between thumps from the door, 'I think…' He paused to allow for the first splintering of the heavy wood. 'Run away,' he decided.

Repple caught the Doctor by the arm as he strode across the foyer. 'You fear to fight?'

'I fear to lose.' The Doctor shook Repple's hand off him. 'Those aren't people. Not flesh and blood to be stopped with bullets or brute force. Not human like you and…' He reconsidered. 'Like you,' he decided. 'Once inside they'll kill every one of you to get at me. Not you, me. Got it?'

'Shouldn't we telephone the police for assistance?' one of the two old men asked. His companion nodded in agreement.

'What?' The Doctor stared at him in disbelief.

'Yes,' Rose said, 'why not?'

'What?'

'You know,' she reminded him, 'officers and cars respond to all calls.'

'We're past officers and cars responding now,' the Doctor insisted. 'That'll just get more people killed.'

'So what do we do?' Aske demanded. 'Wait here to be ripped apart by these mechanical things?' As if to emphasise the point, a panel of the door exploded inwards. A metal fist thrust through, clenching and unclenching before withdrawing to strike again.

'Clockwork, that's the key,' the Doctor told him, grinning at the pun. 'Clockwork soldiers, and clockwork cats. Technology that doesn't stand out, that can't be detected, that isn't out of time and place.'

The door was splintering now. The two knights were clearly visible through the holes punched in the panelling. One of them reached in and scrabbled for the bolts, drawing them back. The lock would not hold for long. Already the metal was screeching and straining with every thump.

'Mr Pooter,' Rose said quietly. 'He's behind this, isn't he?'

The Doctor shook his head. 'No such person.'

'I've seen him. The trustees or whoever they are had a meeting with him.'

'With someone,' the Doctor corrected her.

'What are you talking about?' Repple demanded. 'You say you won't stand and fight, yet any moment now you will have to.'

The Doctor turned full circle, taking in each and every one of the people gathered in the foyer. 'It's me they think they want,' he said. He pointed at Crowther. 'You and your chums, back to the kitchens. If there's no one trying to get in there, get the back door open.'

'You think there might be more of them?' Rose said.

'Or Miss Melissa. They don't want us just walking out the back as they come in the front. That'd be a bit daft.' He turned back to Crowther. 'When and if it's all clear, leg it. If we're not after you in half an hour then we're not gonna be.'

Crowther nodded. He was looking pale, but otherwise calm and in control. The two servants with him were less composed. One of them, he couldn't have been much older than Rose, looked close to tears.

The Doctor turned next to Wensleydale and the two elderly men. 'You three, back to the Bastille Room. Only one way in, so you can defend yourselves better in there. Let's hope you don't have to. Wensleydale – look after them.'

'Sir!' Wensleydale snapped importantly.

'And where are we going?' Repple asked. He had to shout to be heard above the final splintering of the door as the two knights forced their way through the last of the woodwork. The lock fell to the floor, shattered.

'With me,' the Doctor yelled back. He was running now, holding Rose's hand and leading Aske and Repple up the stairs. 'To see a man about a cat.'

The two dark figures stepped through the shattered remains of the front door of the Imperial Club and disappeared from sight. Freddie was standing, watching. He wondered if he ought to follow. Perhaps he could help the Doctor and Rose escape a second time. Or maybe he should wait in case they came out.

'A difficult decision.'

The voice was quiet, close to his ear. Startled, Freddie turned.

The dark mask was close to his face. Matt black, with silver teardrops under the eyes. The mouth was a smiling slash of scarlet. Freddie braced himself to try to get away. But Melissa Heart's hand closed tightly on his shoulder, holding him still.

'He won't run,' she said gently. 'He won't try to escape. It isn't in his nature. He will stand and fight.' She shook her head, the silvering on the mask catching the light and flickering. 'If you only knew what he is capable of, how many he has killed, you wouldn't be so keen to help him.'

She pushed Freddie ahead of her across the street. 'Come with me,' she said. 'Witness the execution of a mass murderer.'

'They are searching each floor, so we have some time,' Aske reported. 'One of them stays on the stairs to prevent our escape, the other checks each room. Simple, but effective.'

'Driving us to this top floor,' Repple said.

'Unless we sneak out down the fire escape,' Rose pointed out. 'Maybe they haven't thought of that.'

'I expect they have.' The Doctor was lying on the floor in front of the door to Mr Pooter's rooms. He had the panel of the door open, the one where Rose had seen the cat emerge. He had peered into the darkness beyond, and now his arm was thrust inside and he was feeling round. 'Yeah, they've got us just where she wants us.' He pulled out his arm and stood up.

'Anything?' Rose asked.

He shook his head. 'Metal box. Like an airlock. The cat enters the box, box closes. Panel in door opens, cat creeps out.'

'An airlock?' Repple said.

'Oh, I doubt there's a different atmosphere behind there. I think it's to stop something else escaping with the cat.'

'Mr Pooter?'

The Doctor smiled at Rose. 'In a way.' He pulled the sonic screwdriver out of his pocket and aimed it at the lock on the door. 'This should...' He stopped. Nothing was happening. The screwdriver was silent, not working. The Doctor frowned and banged it into his palm several times before trying again.

'Flat battery, remember?' Rose said.

'No battery at all,' the Doctor agreed. 'She took it out.'

'Who?' Aske wanted to know.

'Melissa Heart,' Rose told him. 'She's nobbled it. So what now?'

The Doctor sniffed. 'Something less subtle,' he decided. And shoulder-charged the door.

It took the three of them – the Doctor, Repple and Aske – several attempts, encouraged by Rose, who had to be dissuaded from joining in, before the door finally gave way. It swung open sharply, so the three of them tumbled and sprawled into the room. They picked themselves up and looked round in astonishment.

Rose followed them in. She too was staring round in surprise. 'What is all this?'

The large room behind the door was panelled, like so many others in the building. But the walls were clad not in polished wood, but in dull grey metal. Even the floor and the ceiling were coated with it, like a huge metal box. There was no furniture, and dominating the room was a dark metal control console.

Lights flickered and pulsed, power hummed, dials whirred, meters registered various readings. The front of the console jutted out, like a piano, towards the door. But there were no obvious input mechanisms. A bank of screens above the extended section gave different views that Rose recognised as rooms in the building.

As she watched, the pictures changed, switching from one room to another in rapid succession – like the control room of the CCTV system at work in the shop, she thought. One of the screens paused on a picture of the Bastille Room. The camera zoomed in on Wensleydale and the two old men as they manoeuvred furniture to make a barricade in front of the door. It lingered on Wensleydale, then focused in close-up on the revolver he was holding.

The whole assembly was of a dark plastic-like material. Apart from the screens and various controls and read-outs, the only other colour was a triangle of white against the black under the extended front section. It reminded Rose of something, but she could not think what.

Until she saw the cats.

On one side of the console was what looked vaguely like a wine rack. Except that inside most of the pigeonholes was lying the dark, furry body of a cat. Rose counted over a dozen. Each identical – a black cat with a white triangle of fur under the chin. Just like the console.

'The lead shields the emissions,' the Doctor said, tapping one of the walls. 'Melissa Heart would have detected it immediately otherwise. Same reason for the airlock.'

'But what is it?' Rose said again. 'What's it for?'

'It is monitoring events in the building,' Aske said quietly, nodding at the screens.

'You knew it was here?' Rose asked.

He shook his head. 'The purpose seems evident.'

'Some direct feeds,' the Doctor said, examining the console. 'Shielded, of course. Audio and visual links. Then for specific tasks, or to monitor outside the building, it uses the cats.'

'Which is why they're clockwork,' Rose realised.

'Can't be detected,' the Doctor agreed. 'No power source, nothing anachronistic in clockwork. Just the way that it's applied.'

'And the psycho-killer laser-beam eyes?'

'You can get clockwork radios,' the Doctor pointed out. 'Clockwork torches where you squeeze a handle. Same principle. Just shining a light.'

'Sorry,' Rose said to Repple and Aske. 'This is probably a bit beyond you two.' She grinned to show it was child's play to her.

'This is not powered by clockwork,' Repple said, nodding at the console.

'But I can hear it ticking,' Rose said. She was aware of the sound, but couldn't think when she had first started to hear it. When they came into the room, she supposed.

'There may be some clockwork components. But nuclear emission cells, more like,' the Doctor agreed. 'There's a backup supply cable round here. Give us a hand.'

Five minutes later they were ready. Rose was crouched beside the console, Aske and Repple behind her. On the other side of the machine the Doctor held a heavy, well-insulated cable that he had detached from the back of the controls. The end of it spat and hissed like a snake that had eaten a sparkler.

'Shouldn't be long,' the Doctor told them with a grin. He wiggled the cable happily, showering sparks across the dull metal floor.

Rose heard the footsteps first. The rhythmic beat of the two knights as they made their way up the stairs. As they approached it was impossible to tell which sounds were their internal mechanisms and which the thump of their metal feet on the wooden stairs. Together they stood framed in the splintered doorway – blank and unforgiving figures. The metal of their bodies was as dull and dark as the walls of the room.

The voice could have come from either of the knights. It was impossible to tell, as they gave no movement, no indication. The words were rhythmic, uninflected and mechanical. Rasping, metallic, unemotional.

'Doc-tor you will surr-en-der.'

Rose could imagine an internal pendulum swinging inside the thing's chest, a syllable for each sweep of the weight. Each beat alternately high then low – tick-tocks of speech.

'Give up now.'

One of the knights, perhaps the one that had spoken, stepped into the room. It raised its arms jerkily, and started towards the Doctor, gauntlet fingers clutching as they reached for his throat.

The Doctor stood his ground. He waited until the knight was almost on him, then jabbed out with the cable. He stabbed it into the figure's outstretched hand and sparks exploded from the metal palm. The knight staggered back, blue lightning flashing and echoing round its whole body. It stood absolutely still, but Rose could still hear the rhythmic ticking from inside.

'I'd be careful,' the Doctor said. 'That was just a free taster. A longer blast might seriously damage your health.'

'Like smoking,' Rose added. 'We can arrange that too.' She returned the Doctor's grin. At last it seemed like they had the upper hand.

'Now, I've a few questions,' the Doctor went on, dangling the cable so that sparks dripped to the floor beside his feet. 'Luckily, they won't need long answers. In fact multiple choice is probably easiest. Starter for ten…' He sucked in a deep breath as he considered. 'Let's keep it simple. Where's Melissa Heart? Is she, (a), inside the building or, (b), outside the building?'

The knights did not reply. The Doctor waited, tapped his foot with mock impatience. 'Ding,' he said at last. 'But thanks for playing. Time for another shock.'

'How very true.' The voice came from behind the knights. A voice Rose recognised at once. Melissa stepped past the knight at the door and into the room. But she was not alone. She was pushing a small, frightened figure in front of her. Freddie's eyes were wide and scared, his cheeks damp from his tears.

'I'm sorry,' he said in a small voice.

Melissa thrust Freddie at the knight by the door. It grabbed him by the wrist and held him tight.

'What now?' Aske said, stepping out from behind Rose.

Repple stepped out with him. 'You would use children to fight men? So much for honour.'

'Honour died long ago in this war,' Melissa said. Her black mask was smiling, but her voice was shaking with anger. 'Now, Doctor, put down that cable before someone gets hurt. I don't need to offer you a multiple choice of victims, do I?'

As Melissa spoke, the knight pulled Freddie closer, still holding his wrist. Its other metal hand closed stiffly on the boy's neck.

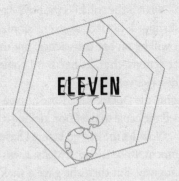

ELEVEN

Freddie's eyes were wide as he stared beseechingly at Rose. She could feel her own eyes watering as the metal hand clamped tighter round the boy's throat.

'Let him go,' she said.

'Doctor?' Melissa Heart prompted.

'Keep hold of the cable,' Aske hissed. 'We have the advantage.'

Rose couldn't believe he would gamble with the boy's life. 'What if she means it?' she demanded.

Aske gave a snort of derision. 'She can't kill him twice. Once he's dead she's got nothing to bargain with.'

'I can't risk it,' the Doctor said, his voice quiet but determined.

Repple pushed in front of Aske, gesturing for the man to step back. 'What sort of woman uses children as hostages?' he demanded. He turned to Aske. 'The Doctor is right. We cannot risk a single innocent life. Lay down the cable, Doctor. We shall take the consequences.'

'But, sire – what if she still kills the boy? And us?'

Repple shrugged, his face as expressionless as Melissa's mask. 'That will be on her conscience, not mine. If she can live with her actions, then let her. But I could not live with mine if we don't surrender.'

'Quite right,' the Doctor said. Rose heaved a sigh of relief as he dropped the cable to the floor, kicking it aside so it was out of reach. 'Now, let the boy go before I have to make you.'

For a moment, Rose thought Melissa was going to have him killed anyway. But then she gave a shake of her head, and the knight released Freddie. The boy stumbled forward, gasping, rubbing his throat. Rose ran to help him.

'I'm touched,' Melissa said, watching.

'That has two meanings,' Rose snapped. 'One of them's true enough.'

'Insult me all you like, girl,' Melissa said in her honeyed voice. 'Now that I have found this butcher, nothing can dampen my pleasure.'

'You don't sound that pleased,' the Doctor retorted. 'Sure it's really me you want?'

Melissa took a step towards him. The knights now flanked her, standing immobile and silent save for the staccato ticking of their internal mechanisms. 'Oh, I am sure now. I did think you were sheltering with Sir George when I heard of this desire to reinstate a deposed ruler. Well, you can imagine what I thought.'

'Nope, wrong,' the Doctor told her.

She ignored him. 'I soon found that Sir George's scheme is the mad hope of a dreamer. He is after all merely human, and his prince is rather more commonplace and earthly than the one I was seeking. A boy,' she said with audible contempt. Rose pulled Freddie into a hug, holding him close and safe.

'Not the murderer I wanted.' Melissa pointed at the Doctor. 'You.'

'Wrong again. Last chance.'

'Then on the way to the dinner, I finally detected the power emissions, as you know. From your quaint sonic device, and from your strange blue box. Then I was almost sure. But there was still a chance that you were not the one I was after. I had to be absolutely sure, you see.'

'Oh yeah. Can't have you killing innocent people by mistake.' The Doctor's face was dark with anger. 'Like that poor maid.'

'Unfortunate.' The mask turned away slightly, and she sounded suddenly sad. 'My friends here don't know their own strength. We didn't mean to kill her, or the other one. Unlike you,' she went on, suddenly angry again. 'Think of the thousands you have killed with your executions, your genocidal cleansing, your disappearances and so-called justice.'

The Doctor shook his head again. 'Ding,' he pronounced. 'Wrong again. If that's all…'

'All?' she screamed at him. 'You murder tens of thousands, and you ask if that is all?'

The Doctor's reply was level and quiet, but edged with anger. 'You've got the wrong man.'

'Have I?' she shot back. She reached into her sleeve and

pulled out a long, slim tube. The cigarette holder that Rose had seen her use in the gallery downstairs. Only now there was no cigarette burning in it, and she was pointing it straight at the Doctor. But when she fired, she was aiming at a different target.

The tip of the tube glowed a sudden red. Then a bolt of fire shot out, blasting into the front of the control console. Screens exploded. Rose and Freddie dived to the floor as glass showered across the room. Freddie shrieked with fright, clutching at Rose. 'Glass!' he wailed in fear. 'Don't let it cut me!'

Aske and Repple both flung themselves sideways. Only the Doctor did not move. The debris flew past him as the main part of the console exploded, but he seemed not to notice. A piece of glass whipped across his jacket sleeve, ripping a hole. He ignored it.

'Missed,' the Doctor said.

'It might be your jailer,' Melissa replied as the noise of the explosion died away. 'It might be programmed to prevent your ever leaving this backward planet, but I know that it is also programmed to defend you. To make sure the order of that jumped-up court is obeyed and your safe exile is not violated.'

'So you destroy a sentient being? Oh, machine intelligence, I know. Not really the same thing.' The Doctor turned and patted the scarred side of the console. 'Even so, I bet that hurt. And all for nothing. I'm not the man you take me for. Though I'll be interested to find out who is. To smoke them out.'

Melissa laughed, though there was no humour or joy in the sound. 'You stand here in front of an AI terminal adorned with the emblem of Katuria and you dare to tell me that you are not Shade Vassily?'

'He isn't.' The voice was quiet, but firm. Repple stepped in front of Rose and Freddie and looked straight at Melissa Heart. 'I am Shade Vassily,' he said.

The Doctor blinked. 'Are you?'

'Of course he isn't.' It was Aske who spoke. He shouldered Repple aside. 'This man is my patient. He has delusions. He believes himself to be a deposed ruler, and now you've given him a name and a cause.'

'What are you talking about?' Repple demanded angrily. 'You know who I am.'

Melissa looked from one to the other, her face inscrutable behind the mask. But the deadly tube she was holding still pointed unerringly at the Doctor.

'They're both mad,' Rose assured her. 'But not as mad as you are if you think the Doctor's some sort of deposed dictator.'

'It was the last action of the Imperial Court,' Melissa said. 'They exiled Vassily before the revolutionaries took control. They should have executed him.' There was bitterness in her voice. 'But instead they sent him to live a carefree life on a primitive planet, with another Katurian as both jailer and bodyguard.'

'To protect him and to ensure he didn't escape from exile?' the Doctor said.

'As you know full well. The records were destroyed, so we

didn't know what planet. We didn't know the jailer was actually an AI.'

'I am Shade Vassily,' Repple said again. 'Can't you see that? How can you not see that?' He was standing erect, one hand on his chest. 'Shade Vassily, Imperial Prater of Katuria. Master of the Seven Heavens. Protector of the Fleet Victorious. High General of Yelkan and Speaker of the Masses.'

Slowly, Melissa swung towards Repple. Slowly she moved her weapon to cover him.

Aske stepped forward, in front of Repple. He held out one hand, a gesture of supplication. the other hand was thrust into his jacket pocket. 'You see how insane he is? I don't know where he has picked that up from, but he's a harmless...' He got no further. With a blur of movement, Aske pulled his hand from his jacket pocket. Rose could see that it was holding a tube, similar to the one Melissa had. The end was already glowing red, and Aske's face had hardened to granite.

Melissa froze. Rose was sure she could see fear in the eyes behind the mask. Just for a second. All the time it took for the nearer of the two knights to turn slightly and raise its arm.

A flash of light. Not a ray, Rose realised, but the light reflecting off polished metal. A blade, spinning at lightning speed across the room. It slammed into Aske's throat, knocking him sideways and backwards. The tube in his hand spat fire across the room, but the shot went wide, merely scarring the dark, metal wall. Aske crashed to the floor, the blade jutting from his neck, blood welling up from the wound.

When he spoke, his voice was a painful gasp. His last words were: 'He's lying. I am Shade Vassily.'

There was silence for almost a minute. Repple knelt beside his friend, checking for a pulse. He shook his head. The Doctor stared at Melissa Heart. Rose hugged Freddie to her, hoping he had not seen what had happened, but knowing full well that he had.

'Well,' the Doctor said eventually. 'Guess that's settled then. If you'll return my blue box we'll be on our way.'

Melissa still held her weapon, still had it pointing at the Doctor. 'I took the precaution of arming the Mechanicals after your escape,' she said. 'Please do not expect me to make any more mistakes.'

'Oh, look, he just told you it was him,' Rose blurted. 'Deathbed confession. Literally. Sorry,' she added as Repple looked over at her.

'Silly question,' the Doctor said, 'but don't you know what this Shade person looks like?'

'I can answer your question, Doctor,' Repple said wearily. He lowered Aske's head gently to the floor and stood up. He stared levelly at Melissa and the two Mechanicals, then turned to the Doctor. 'We Katurians are humanoid, but not human. A Katurian here on Earth would be obvious, and the sentence of the court was that I should be exiled and forgotten. Made insignificant. Dishonoured. My appearance was changed, so that I would fit in.'

'Know the feeling,' the Doctor said quietly. 'Go on.'

'Aske too was altered. He was to be my jailer and bodyguard, as the woman says. He became...' He looked down at the figure on the floor. 'He became a friend, though he rarely let me out of his sight. Oh, I could have my freedom while in exile, provided I never tried to escape. Any explicit attempt and he would kill me. That was his task. His duty.'

'So why admit to being an exiled ruler?' Rose wanted to know. 'If she was after you?'

'How else should I behave?' Repple demanded. 'I am rightly proud of my heritage and my achievements. Aske persuaded me to change the name of the empire I ruled, to scale it back so as not to draw attention, either from the humans or from Katurian revolutionaries.'

'And you did?' Rose said.

'With his hand always on his blaster, how could I refuse? But I will never hide what I truly am.'

'He didn't know we were looking for him,' Melissa said, staring through the mask at Repple.

'Sure it's him then?' the Doctor said. 'Not me?'

She ignored him. 'I could not be certain what planet you had been exiled to or what you looked like.'

'So,' Rose interrupted, 'lucky guess or what?'

'I have friends, people in the hierarchy who have suffered as I have and who still long to see Vassily brought to proper justice.'

'Justice?' the Doctor echoed. 'Oh – you mean, executed. Exile too good for him, is it?'

'Far too good.' The hatred and contempt all but dripped from her words. 'I was quite prepared to search this world and a dozen others until I found this butcher.'

'I brought honour to Katuria,' Repple snarled. 'I built us

an empire, and you fritter it away. Yes, there was a cost. But it is as nothing to the suffering and death your so-called revolution will bring with it.'

Melissa pointed the tubular weapon at Repple. Her hand was shaking, and so was her voice. 'I fashioned my team so they would fit in with the civilisation we searched. And I underwent genetic modification myself, just as you did, so as to fit in.'

'You don't,' the Doctor said. 'Do you? Oh, clockwork knights, OK – nothing too out of the ordinary there. Until they start wandering about killing people of course. But a Painted Lady? Bound to attract attention.'

'It was not deliberate,' she replied sadly. 'There was… a problem.'

'Your operation went wrong?' Repple wondered. 'We destroyed all records of the exile destination and the operations we needed to fit in.'

'The operation went perfectly. The scientists of the revolution are every bit as talented as your hackers and cutters, and I had help from the best of them,' Melissa insisted. 'Don't flatter yourself that because you are safe from the weak-willed leaders who have replaced you that you can escape those of us who know what you are capable of.'

'Then why hide your face?' Rose asked. 'If it is so perfect.' She remembered the rumour that Melissa was too beautiful to look at. Could it be right?

She got her answer. Melissa reached up with her free hand and took hold of the black and silver mask. 'It was a failure of intelligence, of data. Not of technology or talent.

I took information from whatever sources I could beg or buy. I had to assume it was accurate, to take everything on trust.' She pulled away the mask and turned directly to Rose.

Freddie screamed, his head snapping round as he looked away, eyes tight shut. Rose heard the Doctor's sharp intake of breath. Repple took a step backwards. Rose stared back at Melissa Heart, unable to take her eyes off the wreckage of a face. Unable to look away from the grotesque features, the parody of humanity. She could feel her heart thumping in her chest, keeping time with the clicking of the Mechanicals; the blood rushing in her ears as Melissa Heart stared back at her through eyes that now seemed too human.

'This is how we thought you would look,' she said.

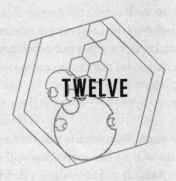

TWELVE

He could hear nothing. Crowther had sent Benjamin away, and told Tom to look after him. The poor lad was almost fainting with fear. No good to anyone. The chief steward had been crouching in the darkened kitchen alone since then, straining to make out what was happening.

There had been the initial sounds of the break-in. He thought he could hear heavy metal feet on the stairs, the measured tread of an inhuman march. But it might have been his own heart thumping in his chest. Or the kitchen clock ticking away the seconds that seemed like minutes and the minutes that seemed like hours.

The longer he waited in the near-darkness, the more he was aware that this wasn't right. He was in charge of the Imperial Club. Whatever was happening here was his responsibility. He was grateful that the Doctor had taken control, and he hoped and prayed that Wyse would soon return. He appreciated Wyse's calm yet authoritative manner, the way the man was willing to help and saw nothing as beneath him. He even spared the time to chat to Crowther about the weather or the latest cricket results. Despite his obsession with chess, he was a real gentleman, was Wyse. And Crowther imagined that the Doctor would be very similar if he got to know him.

He could not – would not – abandon the man to his fate.

In the Bastille Room, Wensleydale stood in front of a pile of furniture. Most of it he had moved himself, with the two elderly men – Ranskill and Coleridge – offering advice and encouragement but little physical help. Wensleydale had sat the old men in large armchairs facing away from the door at the back of the room. If anyone, or anything, did get through the barricade then there was a chance they wouldn't notice the armchairs turned to the wall and Ranskill and Coleridge might be safe. It was a faint hope, but a hope nonetheless.

Wensleydale had no illusions about his own ability to hide. He had no intention of trying to escape whatever fate came his way. He stood facing the barricade, holding his service revolver, remembering several similar moments in his army career. He had survived them all, but he was realistic about his chances. He had seen many good men, good friends, die. Perhaps fate had been saving him for now. If that was the case, then he felt no fear, no anxiety, no trepidation. Just the hope that he would acquit himself with as much honour and courage as his fallen comrades had shown. So, if the creatures, which the Doctor had described as like man-shaped tanks, broke into the room, then Wensleydale's hope was to do them as much damage as he could and protect the old men hiding in their chairs. They were in his care.

But the longer he stood by the barricade, listening for any sign of incursion, the more he resented the passive approach to the problem. There must be some way to take the fight to the enemy without endangering his charges. As he pondered this, as he considered the options, he heard something.

It sounded like a deferential cough from the other side of the barricade. A faceless mechanical killer with a cough? It seemed unlikely. 'Who goes there?' Wensleydale barked.

'Crowther, sir,' came the reply. 'I wonder if you could spare me a minute. I have an idea which I would like to discuss with you. If now is convenient.'

Wensleydale pushed the revolver into the waistband of his trousers, wincing as the metal dug into his stomach. He inspected the barricade for a moment, then heaved at a large chair. It came free, and another chair, several cushions and an occasional table tumbled after it and clattered to the floor. Wensleydale peered through the resulting hole, to find Crowther looking back at him. The head steward looked pale and drawn, a mirror, Wensleydale thought, of his own expression.

'Convenient?' Wensleydale said. 'Well, I don't have anything else on at the moment. What's your idea?'

Freddie had been trying to follow what the grown-ups were talking about. But the metal men scared him, and the sight of the Painted Lady's face was something he knew would haunt his already crowded nightmares. He clung to Rose, and was grateful for the warmth as she hugged him back. He tried not to look at the body of the man at the side of the room. At the blood...

There was movement, behind the metal men. Freddie caught it in the corner of his eye – a brief blur, quickly gone. He stared at the space where it had been, on the landing outside the broken door. Something on the stairs perhaps. A shadow.

The second time, he saw it clearly. A face cautiously rising up. Someone was lying on the stairs, looking into the room, like a soldier looking over the top of a trench. Freddie didn't know who it was – the round, friendly face of a man with slicked-back dark hair. The face was red, as if climbing the stairs had been an effort.

The man saw Freddie looking at him, and a hand appeared – thumbs-up. Then hand and face dipped down out of sight again.

Freddie thought about this. What did the thumbs-up mean? That help was on the way? That everything would be all right? He found Rose's hand and squeezed it, hoping she might understand that he was telling her to be ready, though he was not sure what for. Hoping she might have seen the figure on the stairs and the thumbs-up. But she was watching the other woman – mask thankfully back in place – and she barely glanced at Freddie.

He dug her in the stomach with his elbow, and Rose grunted in annoyance and pain. She glared at Freddie. Freddie nodded at the stairs, as brief and subtle a movement as he could manage and still convey the message. She looked where he gestured. Saw nothing. Wrinkled her eyebrows and forehead into a 'what?' Freddie nodded again. She looked back.

And this time, she did see. Freddie could tell from the way she stiffened. She saw, as he did, the two men creeping up the stairs. One of them was tall and smart in a dark suit. The other, the man who had given the thumbs-up, was so incredibly fat that Freddie almost laughed. He wondered how the man had managed to hide on the stairs, he was so big. But his face was set in a determined expression, and he was holding a gun.

The Doctor and Repple had seen the men too. Freddie could tell by the way their eyes moved. By the way they looked away – looked anywhere except at the men on the landing. The men now stepping into the room.

One of the metal figures swung round, somehow alerted to the threat from behind them. A second later, the other metal man turned as well. As soon as it moved, the fat man leaped forward, surprisingly quickly. He jammed the gun into the Painted Lady's neck. The metal figures froze.

'Well done, Wensleydale,' the Doctor said.

The fat man smiled. 'My pleasure, Doctor. Now Mr Crowther will lead you and your friends to safety while I keep these people here.'

'You won't escape,' Melissa said. Her voice sounded strained.

Wensleydale laughed. 'Oh, I know that. So you'd best be careful, you and your chums here.'

'What do you mean?' Rose demanded. She was pushing Freddie towards the door where Crowther was waiting. The metal men swung round to watch, but made no attempt to stop them. 'You're coming with us.'

Wensleydale shook his head. 'I'm out of puff just coming upstairs. I'd only slow you down. I can't run. But you must.'

The Doctor and Repple were both looking at Wensleydale now. 'There must be another way,' Repple said.

'Let's discuss this,' the Doctor suggested.

'We have discussed it, Crowther and I. You should go. Not waste any more time.'

The Doctor nodded to Rose. 'Go on.'

Freddie was on the landing now. He and Rose and Crowther stood at the top of the stairs. Melissa gave a snarl of anger as Repple moved slowly, reluctantly, to join them.

'We may have to run,' Crowther said quietly.

'Makes a change,' Rose replied.

Wensleydale had relaxed slightly now Freddie and Rose were apparently safe. He turned to the Doctor as Repple stepped on to the landing. 'Now, you leave too, Doctor. No argument.'

The Doctor's mouth opened to reply. But the words never came. As Wensleydale glanced away, at the Doctor, Melissa Heart brought the small weapon she was still holding towards her face. If Wensleydale saw the movement, perhaps he thought it was a cigarette. He hesitated, only a moment. But long enough.

The tip of the tube glowed red. The Doctor's reply became a shout of warning. Fire spat across Melissa's shoulder and caught Wensleydale full in the face. The gun went off. But Wensleydale was already falling lifeless to the floor, and the shot went wide – slamming into the lead panelling on the other side of the room.

'Run!' the Doctor shouted. 'Find Wyse.'

Crowther pushed Rose and Freddie ahead of him down the stairs. Freddie looked back to see the Doctor leaping forwards. But one of the metal knights stepped into the Doctor's path, blocking his escape. Repple was on the landing, looking from Freddie and the others to the Doctor and back. In that split second Freddie could almost see the wheels in Repple's mind turning as he assessed his chances, as he decided what to do.

Then Rose was dragging Freddie with her down the stairs, and the metal feet of one of the Mechanicals were thumping rapidly after them.

The stairs were a blur. Two landings, perhaps three. More stairs. Still the thump of the metal nightmare that was chasing them. It had seemed so cumbersome, so slow. But now it was moving rapidly, gaining on them. It would catch up with them before they reached the ground floor, Freddie realised.

At the next landing, Rose turned to descend the next flight of stairs. Like Freddie and Crowther, she was gasping for breath, glancing back. The metal figure was close behind them now. So close that Freddie thought he could hear its ticking.

Crowther grabbed Rose's arm, pulling her back. 'This way!' he shouted, leading them along the landing, away from the stairs, down the corridor.

'We'll be trapped,' she shouted back. 'There's no way out.'

'Fire escape,' Crowther shouted back.

'We'll never get to it.'

She was right. Freddie didn't know where they were heading, but the Mechanical was almost on them. A metal hand clutched at Freddie's back. He risked a look over his shoulder. It was so close he could see the rivets on the helmet, hear the click and tick of the mechanism that controlled the fingers that snapped and bit at him. He gave an involuntary shriek of fear and looked away.

'Only a few yards,' Crowther gasped.

Ahead of them, on the floor, Freddie could see what looked like a plank of wood, lying across the corridor. Together with the others he stepped over it as they ran. It was only a couple of inches thick.

But as soon as they passed it, the plank rose up in the path of the Mechanical. Freddie caught a glimpse of the old man standing in the doorway at the side of the corridor, holding one end of the plank, lifting it into the path of their pursuer.

The Mechanical slammed into the plank of wood with a splintering crash. The plank had cracked and bent, but it held. The metal man was stopped in his tracks, knocked backwards, and fell heavily to the ground. Freddie caught the briefest glimpse of the Mechanical's fate. He saw the helmet visor jarred free as the head hit the floor. Like Melissa Heart, its mask came away to reveal the lack of a face beneath. Instead there was a mass of cogwheels, clicking round rhythmically. Tiny gears and levers worked furiously. Flywheels spun and mechanisms clicked. Where the forehead should have been, a large multi-faceted glass or crystal stood slightly proud of the mechanisms, catching the light as the creature struggled to stand up. Like the jewelled mechanism of a clock.

Freddie and the others did not wait to see how long it took to recover. Two old men were with them now, already breathless and stumbling. A metal scraping sound from behind them – dragging, maybe the Mechanical clambering to its feet. Freddie did not look back.

There was a room at the end of the corridor, the door standing open. They almost fell inside, and Crowther slammed the door shut, locking it and pocketing the key. 'Well done, gentlemen,' he said.

The two old men were both doubled up, getting their breath back. One of them, Freddie realised with surprise, was laughing.

The other straightened up and looked round. Rose was at the window on the other side of the room, opening it. 'There's a ladder down,' she said. 'Fire escape. Hurry up, that thing will be back in a minute.'

As if in answer, there was a heavy thump on the door. Then another, and a third.

'Where is Wensleydale?' one of the old men asked.

Crowther guided him to the window, where Rose was waiting. He looked back at the door, at the panels that were already splintering and splitting apart. 'I'm afraid Mr Wensleydale won't be joining us,' he said quietly. 'We did discuss this, and he asked me to convey his apologies.'

Rose was waiting for Freddie. She helped him through the window and on to the ladder. 'What will happen?' he asked her.

'We'll find Wyse,' she told him. 'As the Doctor said.'

'I meant, what will happen to the Doctor? And Repple?'

She didn't answer.

Repple looked up from Wensleydale's body. 'And you call me a murderer.'

'I had no choice,' Melissa said.

'There's always a choice,' the Doctor told her. 'Why did you choose to stay?' he asked Repple.

'You are in harm's way because of me, Doctor. I could not abandon you to these... people.'

'And now?' the Doctor asked.

'Now you will come with me back to my house,' Melissa said. The remaining Mechanical stepped forwards, urging them towards the door.

'Tea? How kind.'

'I have a ship ready to take us back to Katuria.'

'No tea?'

'And there you will stand trial for your crimes. Both of you.'

'Both of us?' Repple said.

The Doctor's eyes narrowed as he watched Melissa, waited for her reply.

'It will be a triumphant moment, though overshadowed by the thought of the death, the carnage, the destruction you have caused.' She was staring straight at Repple, through her mask. 'The trial of the hated Shade Vassily, who is responsible for so many deaths.' She turned to face the Doctor. 'And his accomplice.'

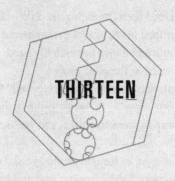

THIRTEEN

The thick glass distorted the murky waters outside. No light filtered down through the Thames, so the glass wall reflected back the image of the Doctor and Repple staring at it. The room was a featureless square, a blocked-off part of the tube that connected the basement of Melissa Heart's acquired house to the airlock of the spaceship she had concealed on the riverbed.

At gunpoint, she and the Mechanical had led the Doctor and Repple from the Imperial Club. The other Mechanical was waiting for them at the house. It gave a halting account of how Rose, Freddie and Crowther had escaped. Melissa dismissed this as irrelevant. She had who she wanted. Now, while she sent messages to arrange an escort and instructed the Mechanicals to begin the power-up procedures, the Doctor and Repple were confined to the space between cellar and ship.

'Fish tank,' the Doctor said angrily. Airlocks were at either end, and two walls of glass. Above them, glass, below them, the riverbed seen through glass. Like standing underwater. He thumped his fist on the transparent wall in front of him. He could feel it give beneath his hand, the mirrored image shimmering as the glass moved.

'I don't think you can smash your way out,' Repple said.

'Not without creating a weak point somehow. Need something sharp to score it, or heavy to wallop it. Preferably both.'

'There is no escape,' Repple pronounced. He stood staring at his reflection. 'I shall face my trial and execution with the dignity of a Katurian noble.'

'Melissa seems to think you're anything but noble,' the Doctor pointed out.

'Propaganda. The revolutionaries have to justify seizing power somehow. They do that by blaming the previous regime – blaming me – for imaginary misdemeanours.'

'Misdemeanours? She was talking about genocide. Whole communities wiped out to preserve your empire. Planets ravaged for daring to question your authority. Thousands of people simply disappearing to suit a political purpose.'

'There are two sides to every event,' Repple replied fiercely. 'Yes, there were rebellions that were put down. Yes, planets tried to secede from the empire. But it was in their best interests to stay part of the alliance and that is what the majority of their populations wanted.'

'So you wiped them out?' The Doctor shook his head, incredulous.

'Of course not. She exaggerates. There were no reprisals, no needless executions. Everything was done with honour and justice. The empire would fall apart if it wasn't based on fairness and the struggle to do what is best. It *will* fall apart now these murderers and mercenaries are in control.'

'You really believe that?' the Doctor asked quietly.

Repple was staring right at him in the glass; his reflected gaze held the Doctor's. 'I do. You saw what she did to Aske.'

'He was trying to kill her.'

'He was trying to save us all.' Repple looked away. 'I should have died in his place.'

The Doctor clicked his tongue and paced out the length of the glass-walled cell. 'Discovering the truth's very difficult when so many people are lying,' he said. 'Even harder if they don't know they're lying.'

'Meaning?'

'That you really believe Shade Vassily, ruler of Katuria with all those titles and long words after his name, is an honourable man. Noble.'

'How else could I live with myself?'

'But Melissa obviously thinks differently. How can you both be right?'

'She is lying,' Repple said. 'Or wrong. Or both.'

'Yeah, it comes down to who I believe. She has the passion, behind that mask. The anger and resentment and commitment. Yet you…' He paused, turned, paced back. 'You stayed to try to help me. You insisted that Freddie not be put in danger. You grieved for your friend, who was also your jailer and might have been your executioner.'

'Thank you, Doctor.'

'For what?'

'For believing me.'

The Doctor's smile froze on his face. 'Don't thank me yet. Your actions are at odds with Melissa's description. Doesn't mean she's wrong, though.'

Repple turned from the glass and pointed at the Doctor. 'So, you think I have changed? Mellowed with my exile? You believe I am a reformed mass murderer?'

'One possibility. But like the truth about you and Aske, several theories may fit the same facts. Perhaps none of them's right.'

'She thinks I was an unjust ruler,' Repple said vehemently. 'That is simply not true. I was deposed by extremists, terrorists with their own twisted agenda.' He jabbed his finger into the Doctor's chest. 'I was not a despot.' Another jab. 'I was not a tyrant.' He was advancing, making the Doctor move back to the glass wall behind him.

At the next jab, the Doctor caught Repple's hand in his own. With his other hand, he jabbed back at Repple's chest. 'You were not a ruler at all,' he said.

'Are you calling me a liar?' Repple cried. 'You think that perhaps Aske was Vassily?'

'No.' The Doctor's voice was calm now, almost soothing. 'Course not. He knew you were Shade Vassily. He died for that belief, his belief in you. He was as sure that you're Shade Vassily as you are. After all, he was sent to protect and guard you, sent to keep you in exile. Given all the facts.' The Doctor shook his head sadly. 'Except one.'

'What do you mean?'

'You know,' the Doctor said, resuming his pacing, 'how

sometimes you only appreciate something when it is taken away from you.'

'You mean my freedom?'

'I mean more like the hum of the central heating or the air conditioning. You only notice it was there when it stops. While it's constant, part of the nature of things, it's unremarkable. Just the way things are. Your brain doesn't even bother to tell you about it, unless there's a change that might be important.'

'Is this important?'

'Like Melissa's Mechanicals,' the Doctor went on. 'If you're with them long enough, you don't even notice they're clicking at you.'

'Your point being?' Repple demanded.

'My point being that it's like the ticking of a clock. You don't hear it, but it's there. Only I have the opposite problem.' He tilted his head to one side. 'Do you hear it?'

'Hear what?' Repple listened for a moment, then shook his head. 'There's nothing.'

'Oh? You see, I can hear – when I bother to listen – I can hear the ticking of a clock. Which is odd. Because…' He paused, encouraging Repple to finish the thought.

'Because there is no clock in here.'

'Exactly. And I've been in this situation before. Several times recently.' He took a step forwards, standing toe to toe with Repple, looking him in the face. 'And always I've been with you.'

Repple said nothing. His face was a blank mask, devoid of expression.

'You're not Shade Vassily,' the Doctor said. 'You just think you are.' And he reached up and took off Repple's face. 'Sorry.' He stepped aside, allowing Repple to see his own reflection in the glass wall behind. 'Really, I am.'

Repple just stared. Stared at the mass of cogwheels that clicked round rhythmically.

'It took me a while,' the Doctor admitted.

Tiny gears and levers worked furiously.

'But I realised I've never seen you smile. Or frown. Or laugh.' He folded up the artificial face and pushed it into his pocket. 'Bit like Melissa, really.'

Flywheels spun and mechanisms clicked.

'Oh, your voice does it. There's inflection and emotion. Very clever.'

Where the forehead should have been, a large multi-faceted glass or crystal stood slightly proud of the mechanisms, catching the light reflected from the glass and the rippling water outside.

'You eat and drink and sleep. But it's all rather mechanical, isn't it?'

Like the jewelled mechanism of a clock.

Repple's mechanised face was at odds with the tortured rasp of his voice. 'I still can't hear it.'

'You live with it all the time. Perhaps they programmed you not to.'

The face turned slowly towards the Doctor. Every part of it seemed to be alive. Only the crystal did not move, but it seemed to as it reflected the light. 'What am I?' Repple demanded. He clutched at the Doctor's shoulders, dragging him closer. 'Who am I?!'

With a whirr of gears and an anguished cry, Repple let go of the Doctor and sank to his knees. His whole body was shaking, as if he were sobbing. But there were no tears, no eyes to cry them.

'Oh, get up,' the Doctor said. 'There's work to be done.'

'There is nothing to be done. No purpose. No reason.' He continued to shake.

The Doctor watched him. 'We don't have time for sulking.'

'What else can I do?'

'Or feeling sorry for yourself.'

The clockwork face turned to look up at the Doctor. 'My whole life is a lie. I am… no one.'

'You may not be Vassily. But you're still Repple.'

'And who is that? Why should I go on?'

'Because if Melissa's right, then somewhere close by there's a power-mad homicidal maniac with a superiority complex who won't let the small matter of the human race get in the way of his escape from this planet. And now that the only thing keeping him in check has probably been damaged beyond repair, he's likely to be making very unpleasant plans to escape, or to rule, or both.'

Repple considered, slowly getting to his feet. His face clicked through the options and possibilities. 'We must tell Melissa Heart. She will help us.'

The Doctor sighed. 'Or she'll decide I'm the villain after all, and you're my jailer. No, we've got to get out of here.'

Repple turned and examined himself closely in the glass.

A mass of cogs and gears stared back at him, the diamond-like crystal that regulated the mechanisms gleamed incongruously in the midst of the machine. 'And how do we do that?' He sounded weary and unenthusiastic.

The Doctor looked at him. 'Use your head,' he said.

He did not wait for a reply. He stepped forward, put both his hands behind Repple's head and rammed it violently forward into the glass.

The crystal cracked into the surface of the toughened window. The Doctor held Repple's head tight, dragging it down and across.

'What?' Repple gasped as soon as the Doctor let go.

But even before he had finished speaking, the Doctor had hold of him again, was smacking his head back into the glass, dragging down and across the other way – through the deep scratch he had already made.

When the Doctor let go again, Repple wrenched himself backwards. In front of him, in the glass, he could see the Doctor grinning, his glee marred only by the deeply scored X that ran through his reflection.

'The weakest point,' the Doctor said, 'will be here.' He stepped up to the glass and tapped on the centre of the X where the two lines crossed. He turned and winked at Repple. 'Brace yourself,' he said. 'Now it's my turn.'

He turned back towards the glass, felt carefully over the window. They could both see that the glass was bulging slightly inwards where it had been weakened. There was a sound like ice cracking. The Doctor nodded happily and took a couple of paces back from the glass. Then he ran at the window. He leaped, legs extended, both feet crashing into the wall at the same time, right in the centre of the X. Crashing into, and through.

Murky, cold Thames water swept in, punching aside the remains of the window and taking the Doctor with it. He cannoned into Repple, and they both fell into the rapidly rising water.

'What now?' Repple shouted, his voice all but lost in the thunder of the hammering water.

'I can hold my breath for ages,' the Doctor gasped. 'And you don't need to breathe.'

One of the airlocks, the door back into the house, not built to withstand the stresses of deep space, buckled under the water's attack. It was sagging, bending, breaking under the pressure of the water. Suddenly it gave way, exploding inwards to allow the water to crash through and along the short corridor the other side towards the cellars of the house.

The corridor sloped upwards, the Doctor remembered as he and Repple were carried along by the immense wave. If they could survive the battering, if he could hold his breath for long enough, they would be washed into the house. His shoulder slammed painfully into a wall, the water rising over his face and the light fading. As the blackness closed over his head, he felt the heavy weight of the water bearing him down and began to lose consciousness. He might not need much breath, but he could still drown, he thought... As the darkness swept over him.

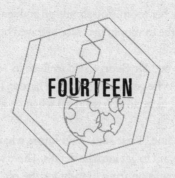

FOURTEEN

Rose's first move, once they were clear of the club, was to make sure that Freddie and the others were safe. Then she would think about how to find Wyse. Crowther had no idea where the man might be except that he played chess every Wednesday evening at a friend's somewhere on or close to the Victoria Embankment. Perhaps Sir George would know.

This was the argument she used to persuade Freddie to go home. Now that he was over the fright, he was keen to find and help the Doctor. Though she could hardly blame him, as she felt the same, Rose, with the help of Crowther and the old men, Ranskill and Coleridge, managed to persuade the boy that it was best for everyone to head for his home.

Dickson opened the door almost immediately. He was visibly relieved to see Freddie and at once ushered them all into the drawing room. Sir George was there already, looking pale and tired. He said nothing, but hugged Freddie tight.

When he eventually let the boy go, he said quietly, 'Your

mother is in her room. You should go and see her. She's worried.' Only the tremor in his voice betrayed how worried she must be.

'Thank you,' Sir George said to Rose as soon as Freddie had gone. 'As he gets older it will get harder, I know. But it is difficult not to be so very worried when he wanders off like that.'

'He was fine,' Rose said. 'You know what kids are like.' She didn't want to get into the details. There wasn't time.

Dickson was pouring brandy for the old men, Ranskill and Coleridge. Crowther was dithering, evidently feeling he should help. Sir George was looking at Rose.

'You all right, my dear?' he asked. 'You look a bit…'

'I am a bit…' She sighed. 'Look, they'll tell you all about it. But I've gotta dash. Have to find Wyse. You don't know where this Ben someone he plays chess with lives, do you?'

Sir George was shaking his head, puzzled. 'Don't know Wyse, I'm afraid to say. Only met the chap a couple of times. Sorry I can't help.'

'Never mind.' Rose all but ran to the door. She turned, aware that they were all watching her.

'I'll come with you, miss,' Crowther offered.

She shook her head. 'I'll be OK. You get your breath back.' She smiled. 'And thanks for what Mum would call the Seventh Cavalry impression.' He obviously didn't understand what she meant, but Rose hadn't got time to explain. 'See ya,' she said.

The moon was struggling to get through the layer of cloud and the gathering fog as Rose reached the river. She felt cold and damp and worried. She would have been more worried if she had seen the figure following her, running quickly between the deepest shadows. Once she turned, feeling for some reason she was being watched. But though she stood for almost a minute, she saw nothing and no one. Getting jumpy, she decided, and continued.

She could remember running along the same stretch of the Embankment before, with the Doctor, soon after they first met. It was strange how similar and yet how different it all seemed. The skyline was lower, yet most of the landmarks were there – the Houses of Parliament, the bridges. No Millennium Wheel, though, she thought with a smile. But the smile faded as she realised that she was putting off deciding what to do, how to find Wyse, helping the Doctor. Maybe she should knock on the doors of every residential house she could find and ask for Ben.

Looking round, wondering where exactly to start, Rose caught sight of movement. Perhaps she had been followed. But no, the movement was ahead of her, moving away – towards Parliament Square. A patch of shadow at first, shapeless, small, barely visible. She ran towards it, keeping to the darkest parts of the pavement, trying to make no sound.

It was a cat. Limping along, back leg dragging. Even from twenty yards away, Rose could hear the unhealthy grinding of the mechanism. It was in a bad way, damaged, she assumed, when the AI system was blown up by Melissa. But it continued to stagger onwards, with a sense of purpose, of direction. It was heading somewhere, and Rose wanted to know where.

The figure behind Rose watched both her and the cat. It nodded with satisfaction.

'Dickson told me Freddie was back.' Anna looked old and frail, obviously affected more than Sir George by her son's disappearance.

Sir George hurried over to her, led her to a chair. 'Sit down, sit down. Yes, the boy's fine…' He frowned, suddenly worried. 'I sent him up to you. Must be quarter of an hour ago now. Perhaps he didn't like to wake you.'

'But I've not been asleep. I couldn't settle. I haven't seen him.'

Sir George sat down heavily beside his wife. 'Oh, my dear,' he said, grasping her hand. 'Oh, Freddie, what have you done?'

The world swam back into existence. The Doctor blinked and stretched. He felt cold and wet and confused. Just for a second. Then he leaped to his feet and looked round. He was standing in a few inches of muddy water in the vaulted cellar of Melissa Heart's house.

Repple was sitting at the bottom of the stone steps that led up into the house. 'I thought you were dead,' he said.

'So did I. How long was I out?'

'A minute. No more. The water washed us in here, then receded.'

The Doctor considered this. 'I was sinking, drowning. No way I'd have made it.'

'I carried and dragged you.'

'Thanks.'

Repple said nothing. He was staring down at his feet. The cogs and gears in his face clicked through their motions without comment.

The Doctor went over and sat down beside him. His clothes were clinging to him and he was tempted to jump up and down to shake the water off. But instead he said quietly, 'Being human isn't only about flesh and blood.' He pulled Repple's face from his jacket pocket. It was made from a pliable yet very strong material. Some sort of porous plastic, the Doctor guessed. Like everything else, it was sopping wet. So he wrung it out like a dishcloth, and handed it, scrunched-up, to Repple.

The face unfolded in the automaton's hand, uncurling and stretching back into recognisable form. The face looking up at its owner. 'Thank you, Doctor.' He pressed it over the exposed mechanism, blinking his clockwork eyes, moving his clockwork mouth.

'Thank you,' the Doctor replied quietly. He got to his feet and made a cursory effort to brush the mud from his shirt with the back of his hand. 'Shall we go?'

He led the way up the steps. There was a wooden door at the top, closed but not locked. The Doctor eased it open and stepped out. He emerged into the hallway; the door was under the main staircase. The Doctor stepped forward to allow Repple to follow. He stood in the middle of the hall, puddles forming round his feet, tapping his chin with his finger as he worked through the possible next moves. 'Do we go or do we stay?' he whispered to Repple.

'And if we go, where do we go?'

'To find Rose.'

Repple touched the Doctor's arm – a very human gesture. 'She will be fine,' he said. 'I'm sure.' There was genuine concern in his voice, between the faint clicks of his mind.

'I know. I'm sure too.' The Doctor smiled thinly. 'Well, 99.99 per cent sure.'

Repple nodded.

'It's just the hundredth of a hundredth,' the Doctor said, 'that's so difficult to accept.' He led the way to the front door, unlocked it, drew back the heavy bolts. Opened the door.

To reveal the faceless metal mask of the huge figure standing outside. It stepped forwards as the Doctor and Repple both turned to run back into the house.

But the other Mechanical was walking stiffly along the hallway towards them, cutting off their escape. The only other route was up the stairs. But at the bottom of the main staircase, where perhaps she had been for some time, sat Melissa Heart.

She was wearing her angry face.

The cat limped its slow way along the pavement, and Rose followed. Freddie watched from the shadows, being careful not to let himself be seen. Rose would take him straight home again, he was sure. And he could help, he knew he could. He owed it to his friends, to Rose and the Doctor, to help in any way he could.

At some point he would have to step out into the light and show Rose he was here. But now she was busy following the cat. Perhaps when they arrived at wherever the cat was leading them...

As they reached Westminster Bridge, the cat seemed to gather itself before making its hesitant way across the road as fast as its failing legs could take it. There was a set of railings across the road on the other side. It managed to climb up and through, dropping down beyond. Rose was across the road in a flash. Freddie followed, but he had to wait for a cab to pass. It sounded its horn in the fog, a melancholy sound, all but swallowed by the heavy air.

Freddie hurried over the road, afraid he might have lost Rose. The smog was closing in now, so that everything was pale and drained of colour. He looked all round, but there was no sign of Rose. He ran to the railing, and leaned over. There she was. As he leaned, the railing moved, and Freddie realised it was a gate. He eased it open and followed Rose down the steps the other side.

A large figure was looming up out of the darkness. Freddie saw Rose duck into cover as it approached. There was nowhere for Freddie to hide, so he crouched down, against the steps, and hoped the figure would not see him.

It was a policeman, he realised as the figure paused at the bottom of the steps. For a moment, Freddie was afraid the policeman was going to come up to the street – and find him. But then the figure moved on, disappearing into the misty darkness as he moved away from the lamp at the bottom of the steps. Freddie hurried down, and across a small lawn. He was outside a large building, could see its impressive silhouette against the pale glow of the moon.

The Houses of Parliament. Staring up at the dark shape, he almost ran straight into Rose. She was standing still, at the edge of the lawn. Freddie managed to stop before he went into her. He held his breath, sure she would hear the thumping of his heart. But she did not move, did not turn. Had she found the mysterious Ben? He could just see the dark shape of the cat dragging itself through an arched doorway on the other side of the path.

Incredibly close, barely muffled by the gathering fog, the hour began to strike. Freddie looked up, towards the sound, mirroring Rose's stance a few feet away. She too was staring up at the enormous clock tower rising high above them. The illuminated face of the clock above the Houses of Parliament shone defiantly through the fog.

He heard her voice clearly between the chimes of Big Ben.

'Oh, you have to be kidding,' Rose said.

Repple stood in front of Melissa. 'You showed me your face,' he said. 'Let me show you mine.' He put his hand to his cheek, pinched at the skin, and pulled his face away from the mechanisms beneath.

Melissa's artificial expression did not change. But her eyes seemed to widen in the mask, and she gave an audible gasp.

'It surprised Repple too,' the Doctor assured her. They were standing at the bottom of the stairs, flanked by the two Mechanicals. Melissa was standing on the staircase, so that she was looking down at them.

'I don't understand,' she said. The angry face turned towards the Doctor. 'You have tricked me!'

He shook his head. 'Not me. I knew nothing about all this.'

Melissa waved the Mechanicals away, and they stepped back from the Doctor and Repple.

'Thank you,' the Doctor said. 'I did wonder if Vassily was actually dead,' he went on. 'Whether this –' he pointed at Repple's face – 'was a charade to allow justice to be seen to be done.'

'Could it be?' Melissa wondered. 'Was Shade Vassily actually killed in the revolution? Or did he take his own life when he saw all was lost?'

'I did wonder. But if that was the case,' the Doctor went on, 'what's the point of the AI terminal at the Imperial Club? No,' he decided, turning to Repple, 'you're a decoy.'

'A decoy,' Repple echoed. He pushed his face back into position as he considered this.

'So was Aske. Both of you were sent here to draw out any assassins who might find Vassily's prison. Who might get too close. Neither of you ever suspected the truth. I'm sure Aske believed absolutely that you were Shade Vassily.'

'And the real Vassily?' Melissa demanded.

'Still hiding. Monitored and protected by the AI.'

'But the AI has been destroyed.'

The Doctor grinned suddenly. 'The cats probably have some level of autonomy, but yes, you're right – the AI's done for. Cats can't do much without it.'

'So, who is Shade Vassily?' Repple said quietly. 'Do you know, Doctor?'

'Can't be certain, but it does seem likely…'

'Yes?' Melissa said, impatience and anticipation meeting in her tone.

'That Shade Vassily is Mr Pooter.'

'But there is no such person,' Repple said.

The Doctor thrust his hands into his pockets, and grimaced as he found the pockets were full of water. 'Oh yes there is. I didn't want to believe it, but...' He sighed. 'We're meant to think there isn't – the daft name, the fact hardly anyone ever sees him. But he's around. And we've got to find him.'

'Why?'

'Because he is a mass murderer,' Melissa told him. She took a step down, looking at eye level at Repple. 'Whatever they might have programmed you to believe about him, he is without honour or compassion. A war criminal with tens of thousands of deaths behind him. Including,' she went on quietly, 'my brother and my parents.'

'More pragmatically,' the Doctor said to Repple, 'how did you arrive here?'

'In a ship. A spaceship.'

'And why didn't you leave?'

'Because Aske would have killed me if I tried. And because the ship was powered down after it was hidden. The cells completely depleted.'

'Ion cells?' the Doctor wondered. Repple nodded. 'Ion cells that would need to be re-energised.'

'Hydrogen extraction,' Melissa said quietly.

'Seems likely.'

'But he would need a supply of hydrogen.'

'And where's the ship?' the Doctor asked. 'Under the Thames, like Melissa's?'

Repple nodded. 'H_2O,' he realised. 'He could energise the Thames to recharge the ion cells.'

'He's had a lot of time to plan how to do it too,' the Doctor said. 'Though the cat would have stopped him from carrying out his plan. Until now.'

'The cat?' Melissa said.

The Doctor nodded. 'The real jailer and bodyguard, controlled by the AI, watching all the time.'

'But now the AI has been destroyed,' Repple said, 'there is nothing to stop him. He may already have the equipment set up, even though he could not use it until now.'

Melissa took another step forwards, standing between the Doctor and Repple. 'And if he energises the Thames, the ozone fallout…'

'Will ignite in the oxygen-rich air and create a firestorm,' the Doctor finished. 'It'll burn through London – every building, every tree, every man, woman and child – in less time than it takes to sneeze.'

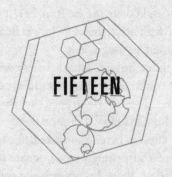

FIFTEEN

Through the arched doorway, there was a view of the courtyard beyond. Inside the base of the tower was another door, off to the right, up a step. Rose followed the cat as it limped its way to the door. It was a modest wooden door with a glass panel in the upper half and a polished wooden plate that said simply, 'The Clock Tower'.

The cat was standing in front of the door, staring at it. It hissed as Rose approached. She hesitated, waiting for the eyes to flash and the deadly rays to lance out at her. But the cat's green eyes seemed dulled and watery. It looked up at her weakly. It didn't seem to have the strength even to extend its claws. On an impulse, Rose knelt down and scooped up the cat in her arms. It was cold and hard under the thin fur. Nothing at all like a real cat, she thought.

'Ah, there you are.'

The door to the clock tower had opened without her noticing. A figure stood in the doorway, the light behind so that Rose could not make it out. The figure stepped down, reaching out and taking the cat from her. It was Wyse. His face creased with amusement as he cradled the cat in his arms and clicked his tongue at it.

'Daft old thing,' he said. 'Must have followed me here.' He held it so he could see into the cat's dull eyes. 'Doesn't look quite the ticket, does he?' He stepped back through the door, nodding for Rose to follow. 'Come on then.'

'You play chess in here?' Rose asked. She found herself at the bottom of a surprisingly small, square stairwell. Stone steps spiralled up above her so high she could not see the top.

'In a manner of speaking.' Wyse looked up with her. They stood close together in the confined space. 'There are 334 steps up to the belfry. Another fifty-nine to the lantern above. I have counted them many times.'

'But – what are you doing?'

He laughed. 'Come and see.' He opened the door again and, in a sudden violent movement, flung the cat outside. Rose heard the metallic thump as it hit the ground. She thought she heard the tinkle of breaking mechanisms. But Wyse pulled the door firmly closed, squeezed past Rose and started up the stairs.

Rose made to follow him up the steps. Then she stopped, hesitating at the bottom. There was something about the way that he had been holding the cat that unsettled her, even before he had thrown it aside so carelessly. The way he rubbed his knuckles into the fur on top of the cat's head, making its brow wrinkle like his own. It seemed so familiar that she assumed she had seen him do it before.

And then she realised that she had. In the boardroom, with the trustees at the meeting. It had been Wyse sitting at the head of the table.

'You're Mr Pooter,' she said quietly.

He turned and looked down at her from several steps above. 'Yes,' he admitted, 'I am.'

'So, you own the Imperial Club.'

'Yes, I do. But…' He shrugged. 'I'm modest about it.'

That didn't ring true somehow. 'Why?' Rose asked.

Wyse had already turned away and started up the steps, obviously assuming she would follow. His voice echoed down to her. 'Because I don't want to attract undue attention. I like the authority, the power, but I would rather not be seen to be wielding it. In short, I don't want to be found, that's why.'

Slowly and quietly, Rose moved back to the door. Gently and carefully, she turned the handle. But the door refused to open.

'It's locked,' Wyse's amused voice came from the floor above. 'You won't get out. So you might as well come up here. Oh, and no one will hear or see you, so don't worry about that either.'

Rose was staring through the glass panel in the upper part of the door. Wyse was probably right. No one would hear. 'Help!' she mouthed. 'Find the Doctor.'

Freddie didn't need to hear. He was standing close to the other side of the door watching her carefully. He nodded. And as Rose started to ascend the stairs, Freddie turned and ran.

Wyse was waiting for her round the first full turn of the stairs. There was a small landing and a door. It was shut. On the opposite wall was a narrow, arched window covered with metal mesh. Rose spared it only a glance – it was obviously too small for her to climb out of, even if she was willing to risk the long drop to the ground outside.

Wyse led her up to the next level, and the next, past another closed door, then on to the next. And the next. By the sixth floor, Rose's knees were aching. She stopped and sat down outside the door.

Wyse had also stopped and was looking down at her in amusement. 'It gets easier with practice,' he assured her. 'Storerooms and offices,' he explained, nodding at the door. 'Most of them empty. Unimportant. Ten of them on top of each other. This stairwell rises up in the corner of the tower. In the opposite corner is a ventilation shaft to draw the stale air through from the debating chambers. Believe me,' he went on with a benign smile, 'when Parliament is sitting there is a lot of stale air to be ventilated.'

'Where are we going?' Rose demanded, getting to her feet again.

Wyse was already on his way. 'The prisoner's room. Not far now.'

'Prisoner's room?'

'Oh, it doesn't refer to you. At least, not yet. It's where naughty Members of Parliament are locked up if they misbehave. Or, in one notable case, if they refuse to swear loyalty to the monarch in the sight of God. Amusingly arcane, don't you think?'

'Hysterical.'

Wyse stood aside to allow Rose to enter the room first. It was a strange shape, more like a corridor than a room. As she walked round the three sides, Rose realised this was because it was built round a square central shaft. But the shape of the room was not as interesting as what was in it. To get round, Rose had to squeeze past the enormous cog-wheels, shafts, gears, levers and dark ironwork. They were dripping with thick, greasy, black oil. But the enormous mechanisms were silent and still – not a click, not a movement. Nothing.

'The clock's stopped,' Rose said. Her voice echoed round the room.

Wyse's laughter echoed after it. 'The clock,' he said, 'is a magnificent feat of precision engineering, given the technology of this rather backward planet.' His monocle caught the light as he regarded her closely through it.

'Oh, you admit you're an alien then?'

He ignored her, continuing as if she had not spoken. 'But the clock is only about the size of a modest dinner table. It will provide the motive force to start my rather grander mechanism, but otherwise it is entirely coincidental and unconnected.'

'Your mechanism?'

The monocle dropped from his eye, swinging on its thin chain. Somehow this time Rose didn't find it funny. 'Impressive, don't you think?' He waited and, getting no answer, concluded, 'You don't. Pity.'

Rose worked her way back to where Wyse was standing

by the door. 'But what's it for? You're this Shade Thingy person, aren't you?'

'Modesty forbids,' he murmured.

'So what are you up to?'

'Escaping from my exile. The cat, or rather cats, for there were several, as you will have realised, were efficient, but lamentably literal jailers. They had orders to prevent me from reactivating the ship in which poor Aske and Repple and I arrived, all that time ago. Not that they knew I was on board. If I had tried to start this machinery the cats would have killed me. However they had no orders to prevent me from having it constructed in the first place.' He gave a snort of laughter. 'That's why they call it artificial intelligence, I suppose.'

'All this is to activate a spaceship?'

'As I said, impressive, isn't it? The design is all my own, though of course I subcontracted a lot of it to the palace's Clerk of Works. For a modest fee. He thinks it's a system to ensure the absolute accuracy of the clock, poor devil.' Wyse smiled at the thought. 'At the moment, they use pennies. They put them on the top of the pendulum, or take them off it, to shift the centre of gravity. Ingenious, but somewhat primitive.' He stepped up to the main part of the machinery, an enormous cogwheel that all but filled the space between floor and ceiling. 'The mechanism extends upwards to the clock above us, and down through the central shaft to the ground,' he explained proudly. 'All for the want of a decent hydro-energising plant.'

'So, what now?'

'Oh, now I activate the mechanism. When the central spring has been wound to the correct point, it will be activated by the clock. The weights will fall as Big Ben strikes the hour, which in turn will release the mainspring. Then, once these wheels have run up to speed, the power realised will energise the water molecules in the River Thames. That in turn will release the energy that the ship will absorb to power up. And I can leave.' He smiled at the simplicity of it. 'You can come with me if you like.'

'No, ta.'

He shrugged. 'Or you can stay here. And be burned beyond recognition along with the rest of London when the ozone ignites.' He waved his hands as if wafting this small problem away. 'An unfortunate side effect of the process.'

Rose stared at him, scarcely able to believe what he was telling her in such a matter-of-fact manner. 'You're mad.'

He nodded. 'Very probably. But I'd rather be mad and alive and free than...' He didn't bother to finish. 'Oh, I must thank you. You and the Doctor.'

'What for? Playing chess?'

'That was a welcome distraction. The Doctor is almost a worthy opponent. But no, for helping, of course. At first I thought you were the revolutionary assassins hunting for me. So I misled you slightly, I'm afraid, about... Well, about almost everything. It seemed quite jolly at the time. But no, your biggest contribution, aside from drawing the real assassins into the open, was to destroy the AI. I assume that was something to do with you two, probably when the Painted Lady and her Mechanicals attacked the Imperial Club.'

'The cats,' Rose murmured.

'I could never have activated this while any of the cats were fully operational. But now the AI is dead and the cats must have collectively exhausted their ninth lives, I can do what I like. Thank you,' he said again. 'You have set me free.'

The Embankment was the only clue they had, and, as Repple pointed out, he could have been lying.

'You are sure that this Wyse is Shade Vassily?' Melissa said. The three of them, shadowed by the two Mechanicals, were walking quickly from Melissa's house back towards the Imperial Club, and the Embankment.

'Yeah,' the Doctor said. He drew a heavy breath. 'And I sent Rose to look for him.' He shook his head sadly.

'Then we must find him soon,' Repple said. 'If I – he – is capable of the things Miss Heart claims…'

'He is,' she told them. 'And more. You cannot even begin to imagine.'

The Doctor nodded gravely. 'Sadly, I can. Come on.'

He led them more quickly into the fog that now swirled around them. 'Oh, this is no good. They could be anywhere.' He stopped and spun round and round in circles. 'Soon we won't be able to see Rose even if she jumps up and down in front of us. Which,' he added, 'is the sort of thing she might do.'

'Doctor,' Repple said levelly, 'who is that?' He pointed into the fog. A dark smudge did indeed seem to be jumping up and down, approaching in a rush.

'Rose?'

The figure emerged into the pale gleam from the nearest street lamp. Not Rose.

'Freddie!'

The boy was gasping for breath. He bent over, massaging his weak leg. After a moment he looked up at the Doctor. His eyes widened, and he gave a yelp of surprise and fear. Melissa and the two Mechanicals had stepped into view. Freddie grabbed the Doctor's sleeve and tried to pull him away.

'It's all right, Freddie. We're all mates here.'

'We have an understanding,' Repple assured the boy.

'Where is Rose?' the Doctor asked quietly.

'He's got her, Doctor. Got her prisoner.'

'Wyse?'

Freddie shrugged. 'A man.'

'And where are they?'

'Up inside Big Ben,' Freddie said. He was close to tears. 'I tried to get in but it's all locked up. Doctor, she's trapped. We'll never be able to save her.'

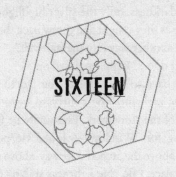

SIXTEEN

It did not look much like a dead cat, not until the Doctor carefully picked it up and straightened it out. An intricate assembly of brass wheels and levers fell from the split fur. It broke apart as it hit the ground, spilling tiny screws and wheels across the flagstones.

'Oops.' The Doctor crouched down and tried to gather the bits and pieces together. 'In a bit of a mess.'

'Can you mend it?' Freddie asked. 'I didn't realise it was a toy, not until the man threw it away.'

'A toy?' The Doctor prodded at the pile of components on the ground. 'I s'pose it is, really.'

'We are wasting time,' Repple announced.

'I agree,' Melissa said. 'We should smash down the door.'

'Yeah,' the Doctor said. 'And have that policeman and scores of his chums round here in a flash. That'd help. We're slammed in pokey and London burns. He'll have made sure that door is very secure. Good plan.'

'You have a better one?' she asked. Her face was almost

lost in the darkness, only the silver highlights in the mask were visible as they caught and threw back the light.

'Must be another way into the stairwell.'

'No other doors,' Repple pointed out.

'Doesn't have to be a door.' The Doctor was walking through the arch into the courtyard beyond, examining every inch of the stonework. Eventually he found what he was looking for. 'Windows – look.' He pointed up triumphantly above the arched doorway, above the roof of the adjoining palace. Pale, thin light was spilling from a narrow window above them. 'That one must give on to the stairwell.'

'And how do we get up there?'

'We climb.'

They climbed.

Melissa instructed the Mechanicals to wait with her at ground level, keeping watch. The Doctor hoisted Freddie on to his shoulders and lifted him as high as he could. The boy clung on to the angled stonework while the Doctor and Repple climbed higher, then the Doctor reached back down and swung up Freddie after him.

It seemed to take an age, but eventually they reached the flat roof of the main building alongside the clock tower. The dark stone stretched up out of sight above them. They could see the pale glow from the faces of the clock almost 300 feet away, but were too close in to see the clock itself. Even at the modest height they had reached, shreds of fog swirled round them in the increased breeze, clammy and cold.

The window the Doctor had seen was at his head height now – higher than Freddie. The boy watched while the

Doctor and Repple examined it, and he heard their disappointed sighs.

'What's wrong?'

'There is a metal mesh over the window,' Repple replied. 'I can probably pull that away, Doctor.'

'Even so,' the Doctor said.

'Even so, what?'

'Too small. Too narrow. We'd never get through there.'

'The cat?' Repple suggested. 'If it can be repaired.'

'That'd take time we don't have.' As he spoke, the Doctor glanced down. Melissa and the Mechanicals were standing below, looking up at them. Blank and expressionless.

Freddie looked back up, and found that the Doctor was staring at him. He lined up his hands with the sides of the window, then lowered them, holding them apart and lining them up with Freddie. It took Freddie a moment to work out what he was doing. Then he went cold with the realisation.

'Just about,' the Doctor said quietly. 'How about it, Freddie?'

Freddie swallowed, his throat dry. 'I'm… not sure.'

Repple was already reaching through the window and tearing away the mesh. It made a sound like a saw cutting into hard wood as it pulled free. He hauled out the ragged mesh and dropped it to the leaded roof at their feet.

Even from where he was standing, looking up, Freddie could see the jagged edges of metal where the mesh had been torn out – sharp spikes jutting from the window edges. 'I won't fit,' he protested. 'I could get scratched. Cut.'

'Give it a go,' the Doctor said quietly. 'Freddie, I wouldn't ask if there was another way.' He crouched down, face level with Freddie's. 'You were a hero for us before, remember? Your chance to be a hero again.'

'Not just for us,' Repple said. 'For Rose.'

'For everyone,' the Doctor agreed. 'All of London. Your parents, everyone.'

'Like Father,' Freddie murmured, remembering the look on his father's face – the mixture of satisfaction and fear and courage. He wondered if his own face looked the same.

'We can't make you, Freddie,' the Doctor was saying. 'We can only ask. It's your choice.'

Freddie sucked in a deep breath, slowly and carefully, afraid it might become a sob. 'I don't want to get hurt,' he said. 'But I'll do it.'

The Doctor grinned and slapped his shoulder. 'Good lad. I'll give you a bunk-up.' He lifted Freddie easily to the window ledge. 'Once inside, see if you can open the door. If not, then go and help Rose. Try to slow down Wyse.'

'What will you do? If I can't get you in?'

'Don't worry. I have a plan. But it will take time.'

It was a tight squeeze. Freddie reached his arms in ahead of him, scrunched himself up as tight and small as he could. He could feel the stone sill hard and cold under him. He could feel the ragged remains of the mesh cover tearing at his clothes, and hoped and prayed he would not get stuck half in and half out.

The Doctor held on to his feet, to save him from falling through the window on to the hard stone stairs inside. It was a drop of perhaps four feet. If he wasn't careful, he would roll and tumble down to the bottom of the tower.

Finally, the Doctor was forced to let go. Freddie's hands were stretched out, but still a foot away from the step below. He fell forwards, his hands smacking into the stone. But he managed to hold on, to save himself from plunging onwards. He felt the remains of the mesh whip at his lower leg as it pulled through the window. His feet slithered down the wall behind.

Freddie sat on the stairs, getting his breath back, scarcely able to believe that he was inside the tower, safe and alive. He rubbed his palms together, inspected them to make sure he hadn't broken the skin, hadn't bruised.

'All right?' the Doctor hissed through the window above him.

'Yes, I think so,' he whispered back. Then he started down the stairs, carefully at first. But then faster and faster as he felt more confident and excited. He was a hero, he was saving Rose and his parents and everyone.

But the feeling did not last. There was no key in the lock of the door. The bolts were firm and he couldn't move them, though he pushed and heaved until he was worn out and had indentations in his sore hands. The Doctor, Repple and Melissa were watching through the glass of the door. One of the Mechanicals had taken a huge swipe at it, but not even made a mark. Freddie had ducked, but the glass was so tough and strong he had not even heard the impact of the blow.

Eventually he gave up. The Doctor had shrugged at him in an exaggerated manner, and smiled, and disappeared from sight. Melissa had also gone. Only Repple was left. He nodded slowly, and pointed upwards. The meaning was clear, and Freddie began the long, tiring journey up the stairs to find Rose.

He was almost back at the window where he had climbed in when he noticed the first spots of blood, glistening red on the pale stone of the stairs. He felt himself go cold, his legs go numb. For several moments he just stared at the thin, scarlet drops that peppered the wall under the window. Then he reached down, without looking, and found at once the tear in his trousers where the mesh had ripped the cloth and scratched his leg.

'Just a scratch,' he said to himself. 'It's not bleeding much. I can save Rose.' He swallowed, but the lump remained in his throat. He blinked, but his vision was still blurred by tears. 'I could be a hero,' he thought, and he stumbled up the stairs, the blood pounding in his ears.

Sitting cross-legged on the ground, the Doctor examined the cat. Lying close beside him was a policeman. It had taken the Doctor a few moments to check that the man was merely unconscious and that the Mechanical that had hit him had not been overzealous. Now the man was snoring loudly, and distracting the Doctor as he worked.

'If I can get this sorted, it can cut through the door for us with its laser eyes.'

'You don't need to fix the whole cat,' Repple pointed out.

'Trouble is I don't know which bit does what. So it's rather hit and miss.' He pulled his sonic screwdriver out of his jacket and aimed it at a collection of cogs he held carefully in place with the other hand. 'Bit of soldering…' Nothing happened, and the Doctor sighed.

Melissa was standing close by, watching through her mask. She stepped closer, holding out her hand. 'Is this what you need?'

The Doctor took the power pack with a grateful grunt. 'Ta.' He popped open the end of the sonic screwdriver and pushed the cylindrical power pack inside before snapping it closed again.

The device whirred, thin trails of smoke rose like mist from the inside of the cat. It flinched visibly, then was still again. The Doctor finished his work and inspected it carefully. 'Might be enough.'

'And if not?' Repple asked.

'I'd need more components for a proper job. You know an all-night watchmaker's?' He tugged the fur round the cat's metal-frame body, then he got to his feet, holding the cat out in front of him. 'Come on, kitty-kitty.' Nothing. He shook the cat. 'You know what we need to do, don't you, puss?' Still nothing. He shook it again, and the cat gave a weak, desultory meow. Its head lifted a fraction, its eyes gleamed slightly. Then with a whirr and a clunk, the head fell forwards again.

'What components do you need, Doctor?' Melissa asked in the quiet that followed.

'You do know a watchmaker?'

'No. But we do have a ready supply available.'

The Doctor looked at her blank face. Then he looked at Repple.

'You expect me to die for you?' There was the faintest tremor in his voice. 'I don't know if I can, Doctor.'

Melissa laughed. 'I expect nothing.' She raised her hand, beckoning. And one of the Mechanicals stepped out of the gloom. It stopped in front of the Doctor. Slowly and deliberately, it raised one gauntleted hand and slid open the visor that covered its head. To reveal the cogs and gears and mechanisms inside.

'Even machines need something to die for,' Melissa said.

Freddie could hear the faint voice echoing down the stairwell. He held tight to the metal railing on the inside of the stairs. He wished he had his crutch. His legs ached so very much, but he knew he had to keep going. Once he looked down the hole in the middle of the square, and shuddered at the height he had climbed. But he kept going. The voice was getting louder, closer, as he climbed the stairs.

It was a man's voice. Calm and reasonable and under other circumstances Freddie would have thought it friendly. It was coming from an open door on the next level. He slowed, trying to catch his breath, afraid the man – Wyse – would hear his heart beating.

'I was intending to wait for midnight,' Wyse was saying. 'It seemed suitably melodramatic. But I imagine the Doctor will be looking for us by now, so we shall have to settle for ten o'clock, which is such a pity.'

'Big shame.'

'Don't be too upset. That's the only reason you're still alive.'

'Star billing in a hostage drama,' she said. 'Oh, great.'

Freddie could hear Rose clearly. It sounded as if she was just inside the room. He crept up to the door, tiptoeing, ignoring the drip of blood from his leg. The bottom half of his trouser leg was sopping. 'It's just a scratch,' he told himself. He edged closer, and risked a quick look into the room.

Rose was standing just inside. Wyse was beside her and together they were looking at the enormous clockwork mechanism that filled the room. The immensity of it almost made Freddie gasp in awe. For a moment, he forgot his injured leg.

Perhaps it was the movement, or perhaps it was an instinct. Whatever it was, Rose turned, just in time to see Freddie standing in the doorway. Wyse also started to turn, and he ducked out of sight quickly. But in that instant, he had been rewarded with Rose's smile, her realisation that she was not alone. It made everything worth it. Freddie braced himself, wondering what to do now.

The cat's eyes glowed and twin beams of light shot out from them, focusing on the area round the lock of the door. The light ate into the woodwork with a screech of power.

After a few moments, the lock like the bolts before it fell away and the door swung open the smallest fraction. The Doctor dropped the cat to the ground and kicked the door open fully. It crashed back into the wall behind. The Doctor was already through and running, followed by Repple and Melissa.

The Mechanical paused in the doorway. It turned stiffly to look back at the inert remains of its fellow – face plate open and mechanisms hanging out. Cogs and wheels and tiny bolts were spilled across the flagstones beside the unconscious policeman.

Then the Mechanical turned and followed its mistress into the clock tower.

By which time the cat was gone.

As he waited, listening to Wyse talking about things he did not understand – about ionisation and ozone and potential energy and space – Freddie leaned against the stone wall. His mind swam, the effort of the climb catching up with him perhaps. He shook his head to clear it, and caught Wyse's words from inside the room.

'Sadly, I need to prime the clock itself in order to set this rather impressive mechanism in motion and begin the process.' The voice seemed closer now. 'And the clock is above us. If you would care to lead the way?'

Rose emerged from the room first. She glanced at Freddie as he pressed himself back against the wall, then turned quickly away and started slowly up the next flight of steps.

Wyse followed. He paused in the doorway. Freddie held his breath. But Wyse was already turning to follow Rose. Freddie would have to move quickly. He would have to get into the room and out of sight before Wyse turned the corner of the stair and saw him. Freddie braced himself.

As he stepped out of the room, Wyse slipped. Only slightly, one foot sliding forwards a few inches on the stone floor. Enough to make him look down. Look down and see the trail of fresh blood that his foot had smeared across the threshold. He frowned, started to turn towards Freddie.

At the same moment, a noise echoed up the tower. A sudden powerful screech followed by a sizzling like hot metal plunged into cold water. Then the bang of the door at the bottom of the stairs as it crashed open.

Freddie was staring right at Wyse. He saw the man's face crease into a frown, then surprise, then anger. 'The cat?' he murmured.

It was now or never. 'Rose!' Freddie shouted.

Already she was running back down the steps, already she was pushing Wyse away, into the room behind him. She grabbed Freddie's hand and they started down the staircase.

Then she shrieked – surprise and fear rolled into one sound.

Wyse had hold of her hair – had grabbed it as she rushed past, and was dragging her back.

'Run!' she hissed at Freddie, eyes wet with tears of pain.

But he held on to her hand, shaking her head. 'I can't.' His voice was almost a sob.

Wyse dragged her back, then thrust her ahead of him up the stairs. He reached down and grabbed Freddie by the shoulder and shoved him after Rose. 'Quickly,' he urged. He pulled a small revolver from inside his jacket, and jabbed it at them. 'Hurry, or there'll be more blood on the stairs.'

'The Doctor will stop you,' Rose said, her tone oozing confidence.

But Wyse laughed. 'Once I start the mechanism, nothing can stop it. Besides…' He paused to shove them into another room. 'I now have two hostages.'

The centre of the clock room was dominated by the clock itself. Wyse was right, it was hardly bigger than a dinner table – a flat ironwork bed on which the heavy metal mechanism was laid out. Levers and wheels led up to huge rods that reached out and through the walls – to turn the hands of the four clock faces outside. The heavy persistent tick of the mechanism echoed round the room.

Freddie slumped in a corner away from the clock. Rose was beside him. Wyse was at the clock, clicking a lever into place and smiling. From somewhere far below came a heavy grinding sound.

And then the Doctor was standing in the doorway. His face dark, his eyes cold. 'Let them go.'

Wyse laughed. 'Come in here and I will kill them.'

'Let them go, or you will never get to your ship.'

'You leave, Doctor. Then I shall go to the ship. Then you can come back for them, if you have time. The clock has already struck the quarter. When it reaches the hour…' He waved the gun by way of demonstration.

'He would rather die than surrender?' It was Repple's voice from the stairway outside.

'Yes, he would,' Melissa answered.

Wyse too had heard them. 'You can't stop the mechanism,' he insisted. 'And when the clock strikes…' He stopped abruptly, as if surprised at his own words.

'When the clock strikes,' the Doctor echoed. There was the ghost of a smile on his face now. 'What if it *doesn't* strike?'

Then he was gone in a blur of movement. The door slammed shut.

Wyse cried out in anger. 'You can't stop it.'

'Bet he can,' Rose said. She was grinning.

Wyse looked at her, assessing the situation. Then he ran across the room. Holding the gun poised, he pulled open the door. The stairway was empty.

'Stay here. And I wouldn't try to stop the clock. If you do, the spring will activate and the weights will drop and start the process immediately.' Then he was gone. The door slammed shut and a key turned in the lock.

Rose was on her feet. 'Come on,' she said. 'Maybe we can stop the clock without setting it off.' But, looking at it, she sighed. 'Dunno where to start.'

'Anywhere,' Freddie suggested weakly.

'But I might set things off when the Doctor's just about to stop it,' she said. 'We'll be OK. He'll sort it.' She turned to smile encouragingly at Freddie. But the smile froze.

'You're bleeding.'

'It's my leg. I caught it on the window when I climbed in.' He stretched it out and she ran over, pushing up his torn trouser leg to reveal the skin slick with blood beneath.

Rose rubbed at the blood, trying to see where it was coming from. 'It's just a scratch,' she said with relief. 'It's not that big or deep. Keep still, and it'll soon stop bleeding.'

Freddie shook his head. He felt pale and woozy. 'No it won't,' he told her. 'Mother says it's her fault. In her blood. Sir George says it's proof of who I really am.' His eyes were moist as he stared up at Rose. 'When I start to bleed, I don't stop.'

SEVENTEEN

The Doctor was gone. But Repple and Melissa were waiting on the landing below when Wyse emerged from the clock room and slammed the door shut behind him. Melissa stepped forward as Wyse glanced down.

'Vassily!' she shouted.

He looked straight at her as she raised the tubelike weapon and fired.

Stonework beside the door, close to Wyse's head, exploded into stinging fragments. He barely flinched, took his time, aimed the revolver.

The crack of the gunshot echoed loudly in the confined space. Melissa gave a shriek of surprise and pain as the tubular device was knocked from her hand by the bullet. A line of red traced across her palm, and the tube tumbled into space. As the echoes died away, Repple heard it shatter on the floor nearly 300 feet below.

Wyse had stepped forward to the rail outside the clock room. He took aim again. On the lower turn of the stairs, the

223

remaining Mechanical raised its arm. The blade caught the light as the tiny knife spun upwards at Wyse. He moved his head just enough to allow it to pass and embed itself in the door behind him. The gun was pointing directly at Melissa.

He fired, turned, and ran in one movement. Melissa did not flinch.

But Repple did. He leaped in front of her, the bullet catching him in the chest, driving him backwards down the stairs. He slumped to the floor, close to where Melissa was standing. Her expressionless face spared him a look, then she was off up the stairs, shouting for the Mechanical to follow.

Repple lay there, gasping, listening to the rapid clack of their feet as they hurried after Wyse. He felt for the wound, found the opening the bullet had torn in his waistcoat and shirt. He reached trembling fingers through the ragged hole. And pulled out the flattened lead that had impacted on the flesh-covered metal of his chest. He stared at it.

'Why can't I bleed?' he murmured. Then he tossed the spent bullet over the railing and got to his feet. The bullet clattered off the steps on the other side of the stairwell, then bounced back and into the abyss. The sound of its bounce, clatter, fall and eventual impact on the floor below rang in Repple's ears as he hurried after Wyse. And when the sound was gone, for the first time in his life, Repple fancied he could hear the dull ticking of a clock coming from somewhere inside his own head.

Wyse had only run up one short flight of stairs. Then he ducked inside another wooden door, and pushed it closed behind him. He stood, listening, at the door. He smiled as Melissa and the Mechanical ran past, up towards the belfry.

His smile froze as the Doctor's voice came from behind him: 'Hello.'

The door led into a narrow gallery that ran inside one of the faces of the clock. The whole of one wall was taken up with the clock face – over twenty feet in diameter, over 300 separate pieces of glass held in place by metalwork. A huge rod from the adjacent clock room ran through the wall and into the centre of the clock to drive the hands.

The other wall was a mass of light – bulbs blazing brilliantly to illuminate the clock face, throwing the shadows of the Doctor and Wyse against the opal glass. Just past the six o'clock position a whole large pane of glass had been pushed aside.

Wyse knew it was hinged to allow maintenance access to the clock face – a space barely big enough for a small man to squeeze through. The Doctor was standing beside it, pushing it closed, smiling with self-satisfaction.

'What have you done?' Wyse hissed. He raised the gun.

But the Doctor was already gone, dashing to the end of the room and turning the corner towards the next clock face. Wyse ran after him. He stopped at the centre of the gallery, and shoved open the glass panel. Had the Doctor somehow managed to stop the clock? Was he trying to jam the minute hand before it could reach twelve? Could he really have climbed up the outside of the clock and back again?

He leaned out through the glass. The wind whipped at Wyse's hair, blowing it into a panic around his head. He leaned as far as he dared – as far as he could. But it was not far enough to see where the clock's hands were. If it had been daylight outside he knew he would have seen the long minute hand silhouetted against the glass from inside. Where was it now?

Unable to get further through the panel, Wyse gave a grunt of both satisfaction and annoyance. If he could not get through the panel, then neither could the Doctor. Wyse had fallen for the bluff, had stopped to check and given the Doctor a few precious moments longer for whatever he was really up to. He started to pull himself back inside. And found he could not move.

The Doctor waited until Wyse was leaning through the panel, then ran back and pressed hard against him with both hands, holding him so he could not pull himself back inside. It would not prevent the clock from striking, but it solved one problem at least.

'Melissa!' he shouted as loudly as he could. 'In here, quickly.'

Wyse had realised what was happening and was struggling to get back in. The Doctor could imagine him trying to angle the gun so he could shoot at the Doctor. Even so, the sound of the shot, followed immediately by the crash of breaking glass, surprised him. The bullet ricocheted off the inside wall. Glass snowed down on the Doctor, tearing at his hands and face. He could see the door at the end of the gallery open and the Mechanical starting towards him.

Then the bullet bounced up off the floor and tore through a vital cable. The lights went out, plunging the Doctor into utter darkness.

He had relaxed his grip on Wyse slightly as the glass scythed into his hands. Wyse renewed his struggles, heaving backwards in an effort to break the Doctor's hold. At the same instant, something cannoned into the Doctor and sent him sprawling to the floor – the Mechanical, as confused as the Doctor by the loss of the lights.

There was a pale glow from the next gallery, where the lights were still working. As his eyes adjusted, the Doctor could make out the tall shape of the Mechanical above him reaching for where Wyse had been. But the man was no longer there. The Mechanical stepped back, as if perplexed. The Doctor pulled himself to his feet, looking round in the hope of catching a glimpse of Wyse.

Instead, he caught the full force of Wyse's attack – felt the man's shoulder in the small of his back, forcing him violently forwards into the clock face.

The glass shattered as the Doctor crashed head-first into it. Metal stanchions twisted and broke away. Cold air and clammy fog blasted into the Doctor's face and he felt himself twisting, tumbling, falling. Through the clock. Into space. Three hundred feet above the ground.

No one could hear, she was sure. Rose hammered on the door. She heaved and shoved but without success. Her cheeks were wet and she brushed at them absently with the backs of her hands as she shouted and yelled and prayed for someone to come and help.

'He's dying!' she screamed.

But there was no answer.

In the corner of the room, Freddie's breathing was shallow and rapid. The most accurate mechanical clock in the world ticked away the unforgiving seconds as the blood slowly dripped from his body.

Once the clock struck the hour and the weights dropped, Wyse knew that the process would start. He would have perhaps fifteen minutes to get to the ship before the atmosphere became unstable. Ten for safety. He crept slowly along one of the galleries behind the clock face. The lights still worked here, but he was listening for the slightest hint of a mechanism that was not the main clock.

He had two options. He could go to the ship now, and hope that the Doctor's friends were unable to stop the mechanisms. If everything went according to plan, he would be safe in the ship when she powered up, ready to leave this pathetic planet far behind. Or if not, then at least he was free and able to try again, if only he could escape from the Painted Lady and her Mechanicals.

On the other hand, he could stay until the mechanism activated. He could make sure that everything worked, and still have time to escape to the ship. There was an element of risk, but Shade Vassily was not one to shy away from danger. He had allowed himself to be sidelined once, by agreeing to exile rather than almost certain death. He would not shirk his responsibilities – his destiny – again.

He stepped out of the gallery. He paused to savour the cool breeze from the broken clock face that gusted along the adjacent gallery, and to listen to Rose's screams and shouts for help. The others would surely be paying more attention to her than to hunting for him. He smiled and started up the stairs towards the belfry.

The wind was blowing holes in the fog. The air was still cold and damp, but through the tattered fog there was a magnificent view of London. Under other circumstances, the Doctor might have been impressed.

But just now he was hanging by tired fingers from the bottom of the clock face, struggling to hold on. Under the clock, the tower extended outwards slightly. Hardly a ledge, but enough for the Doctor to have collided with it as he fell. He had bounced, slid, scrabbled, and finally managed to get a grip. Hardly even that. His fingers were latched on to the final edge of stonework. Stonework make slippery by the fog and the London grime that coated it.

One hand slid off. The Doctor frowned. He reached back up, trying to grab hold. But it was too far away. He tried again, reaching as high as he could, feeling the stitching in his jacket give way under the arms. He couldn't possibly die needing a new jacket. The Doctor gritted his teeth, ready for one last try.

His hand swung up again, clutching at the air, finding nothing. At the same moment, he felt the fingers of his other hand slipping from the ledge. 'Sorry, Rose,' he said quietly.

Then his free hand slapped into something solid. Instinctively, he grabbed it, held on tight. And whatever it was held on to him. The Doctor was moving – not falling, but being hauled upwards. A moment later he found himself sitting on the ledge he had been so desperate to cling to. It was surprisingly wide.

Sitting beside him was Repple. 'You looked like you needed a hand.'

'Several.' The Doctor looked up, and saw that it was an easy climb back through the shattered clock face and into the tower. He got cautiously to his feet, and slapped Repple on the shoulder. 'Thanks. I owe you.'

'We must stop Wyse,' Repple said simply as he climbed up after the Doctor.

The Doctor was already easing himself carefully over the broken metal frame and the remains of the broken glass. 'Too right. No time to hang around.'

They stood together in the darkened gallery, feet crunching on the broken glass. The muffled sound of Rose's shouts reached them from the clock room, but it was impossible to make out her words.

'She's always impatient,' the Doctor said. 'You sort out Rose and Freddie. OK?'

'Very well, Doctor.'

They were hurrying along the gallery, back towards the stairs. 'And then see if you can jam the mechanism in the rooms below somehow. Anything to slow things down. Where's Melissa when we need her?'

'I do not know. What will you do?'

The Doctor started up the stairs, taking them two at a time, hauling himself along by the handrail. 'The drop of the weights when the clock strikes is the trigger. He must have a tap into that system, in the belfry.' He disappeared round the corner of the stairs, voice echoing back down, above Rose's shouts. 'I'm going to disconnect it.'

Rose was almost hoarse from shouting. She thought she heard the Doctor calling from outside, and paused to listen. But there was nothing. She looked back at Freddie – he seemed incredibly pale. She tried not to look at the red puddle growing beside him. How much blood was there in a boy's body? Must be several pints. Five, maybe. She tried to imagine how much that was, thinking of when she had dropped a slippery milk bottle in the kitchen. A beer mug knocked over down the pub…

Freddie smiled weakly at her. She tried to smile back.

Behind her, the door gave a massive crack. Rose ran over to Freddie, and together they watched as the wood splintered and broke round the lock. Someone was forcing their way in.

'Friend or foe?' Rose wondered out loud.

The lock gave way with a screech of tearing metal. Screws fell to the floor, followed by the lock itself. The door swung open, and Repple stepped into the room.

'Whose side are you on?' Rose demanded. 'Come to that, just who are you, anyway?'

He strode quickly across to them, and knelt beside Freddie, examining the gash in his leg. 'I am on your side,' he said.

'And I am just finding out who I am.' He looked up at Rose. 'Why isn't this healing?'

'Because he's a haemophiliac. I should have realised.' Only now, only when she said it out loud, did Rose start to cry. She could hear Freddie telling her how his stepfather wouldn't dare hit him – telling her before the boy even knew he was a prince. She could see his mother's tortured face and wondered how she could cope every day knowing the slightest scratch could kill her son. She thought about the one thing people remembered about the Romanovs. That and the fact they were dead. Now her innocent stupidity was killing Freddie.

Through her tears, she saw that Repple had torn away the leg of Freddie's trousers and was using the sodden material as a tourniquet. She hadn't even thought to do that for him.

'It will help,' Repple said. 'But it won't stop it. We need to close up the wound. Cauterise it in some way.'

Rose blinked back her tears and wiped her face on her sleeve. 'Sonic screwdriver,' she remembered. 'The Doctor said it can cauterise wounds.'

'Find him. Get it.'

Repple ran with her to the door, his hand on her shoulder. 'Hurry,' he said quietly, so Freddie would not hear. 'He doesn't have long.'

The stairs led into a large open area at the top of the tower. The bells were hung centrally – the largest, Big Ben itself, in the middle, with four smaller quarter bells clustered round it. There was a wooden platform under the bells, slightly raised from the stone floor that bordered the room. The walls were broken by open arches giving views out over London.

The Doctor ran into the belfry, up and over a small iron bridge that led to the far side of the room. More steps led up to the topmost gallery but he ignored these. On the far side of the room he found Melissa, stooping beside a vast metal grille that covered the whole of one side of the belfry.

'Ventilation shaft,' he gasped. 'They light a fire at the bottom to draw the air through the building.' Looking across they could see the shorter but wider Victoria Tower at the other end of the palace. 'There's another one in there,' the Doctor added with a nod. He looked down again. 'Oh.'

'Yes,' Melissa said, as they both looked into the shaft. It was filled with machinery. 'I did think perhaps Vassily was hiding in one of these shafts.'

'He's really gone to town on this,' the Doctor said.

Melissa straightened up. She pointed across towards the bells, indicating the heavy hammer that was standing slightly proud of the side of Big Ben. 'He has attached a mechanism to the hammer, and thence to the weights.'

The Doctor ran to look. 'Yeah. Tricky.'

'It can be disconnected,' she said, joining him. 'But, as you say – tricky.'

'We've got about five minutes. One false step and the weights fall. Big Ben would sound an early death knell.'

One of the shadows close to the top of the stairs moved, detaching itself from the gloom and stepping up on to the raised bridge over the bell platform. 'Step away, Doctor,'

Wyse said. He was pointing his revolver at them. 'And you,' he added, moving the gun slightly to point at Melissa.

'I'll leave it to you then,' the Doctor whispered.

Wyse was walking slowly along the bridge, keeping the gun level.

Melissa's black and silver mask turned to stare blankly at the Doctor. 'You'd trust me?'

At the end of the bridge, Wyse paused. He could come no closer without moving behind one of the quarter bells, giving them a moment to escape.

The Doctor kept his eyes on Wyse as he replied to Melissa's question. 'You're not a killer. Not really. You'd rather be saving lives than chasing monsters, admit it.' The Doctor gave an encouraging smile. 'We all would.'

'We should not pretend to be what we are not,' she agreed. And Melissa Heart removed her mask.

Wyse froze at the sight of her face. Not horrified, but startled. Melissa ignored him and turned to the mechanism attached to the hammer. The Doctor launched himself across the platform, under the quarter bell, crashing into Wyse's midriff.

The gun clattered to the floor – bounced and tumbled across to come to rest close to one of the arched openings.

The Doctor wrapped his arms round Wyse's legs, bringing him down. A foot broke free and kicked savagely at the Doctor's face. He winced under the impact. 'I'll keep him busy,' he gasped to Melissa. He let go with one arm, and fumbled in his pocket while trying to keep hold of Wyse with the other arm. 'Here, you'll need this!' He managed to draw out the sonic screwdriver, and tossed it across to Melissa.

She caught it easily, and set to work.

The bandage was painfully tight round the top of his leg, but Freddie thought it was helping. There seemed to be less bleeding, though the scratch was still dripping blood into the growing pool beside him.

'I was a hero, wasn't I?' he asked weakly.

Repple nodded. 'Yes.'

'I never knew I was a king. I thought I was just an ordinary person.'

'Yes.' Repple looked away. Freddie thought he was going to say something more, but he was silent.

'That's all I wanted, really. But it's good to be a hero,' Freddie said when Repple said nothing more.

Repple got to his feet. 'I never knew it,' he said, 'but I just wanted to be an ordinary person too. Now it seems we all get to be heroes.' He looked down at Freddie, his expression as blank and unreadable as a mask. 'I have to go now. You'll be all right. I promise.'

'Please – I don't want to be alone. You will come back?'

Repple paused in the doorway. He turned slowly to look at Freddie. 'I will come back,' he said. Perhaps it was a trick of the light, but it seemed to Freddie that the man was smiling.

The Mechanical had methodically checked each of the galleries behind the four clock faces. But it had not found its target. It paused at the end of the final gallery, examining the shape in the shadows beside the door.

Just a cat, limping slowly and painfully back towards the stairs. The Mechanical stepped over it and out into the stairwell. It caught a glimpse of a figure moving quickly down to the lower levels of the tower. It clicked through the possibilities and options, then started down the stairs in pursuit.

Too late, the Doctor realised what was happening. Wyse was dragging him along, crawling across the floor. They had clattered and bumped down the steps from the bridge, and the Doctor was still holding tight to the man's leg. Wyse was stretching out across towards one of the archways. Towards the gun.

The Doctor hauled him away. But Wyse managed to claw back a few inches. His fingers were brushing against the gun. Another few seconds and he would have it.

A face appeared close to the Doctor's – right beside him on the floor. Rose, kneeling down and staring at him urgently.

'I need the sonic screwdriver,' she said. She was snapping her fingers. 'I need it now!'

The Doctor stared back at her. He glanced at Wyse, at the hand closing on the gun. 'Rose!' he said in annoyed astonishment.

'What?' She glanced where the Doctor had been looking. 'Oh. Hang on.' With a sigh, she stood up, stepped over the two struggling bodies, and kicked hard at Wyse's hand as he managed to get hold of the gun.

The gun skidded across the floor, through the archway and out of sight.

'Right.' She was kneeling beside him again. 'Sonic screwdriver.'

'Melissa's got it,' the Doctor managed through clenched teeth. Wyse's fist cracked into his jaw, snapping the Doctor's face round. When he looked back, Rose was gone.

'I need it,' Rose pleaded.

'You'll have to wait.'

'I can't. Freddie's dying.'

'We'll all die if I don't finish this,' Melissa said.

Rose swallowed, trying not to look at Melissa's face. She could grab the sonic screwdriver, wrench it away from the woman and then leg it. But Melissa was right, that wouldn't help. But if she waited...

'Hurry, then!'

Melissa glanced at her. For once, Rose could read every nuance of her expression.

The huge main cogwheel glistened with oil and grease. Repple walked all round it, examining every aspect. Easy enough to jam some of the smaller components. But if this main wheel turned, it would break through everything else. This was where he needed to do the damage. Stop this wheel and everything else would grind to a halt.

But there was nothing he could see that he could be sure would stop the wheel. Nothing that would withstand the enormous force once it started to move. Above him he heard the first chimes of the quarter bells as ten o'clock arrived. With a mechanical groan, the cogwheel began slowly to move, teeth biting into the gears and levers it was designed to operate.

The noise inside the belfry was deafening. Rose could not begin to imagine what it would be like when Big Ben itself struck in a few seconds.

Melissa handed Rose the sonic screwdriver without comment.

'You've finished?' Rose gasped in elation between the chimes.

'No,' Melissa shouted back. 'It is too late.'

The air itself seemed to shudder as Big Ben struck the first chime of the hour.

Rose ran. She jumped over the struggling forms of the Doctor and Wyse. She ignored Wyse's laughter. Her thoughts were only of Freddie. It didn't matter that everyone else was about to die, that the world around her was coming to an end. Only that she save Freddie. For a few precious seconds at least.

'Rose!' the Doctor's voice screamed at her between the chimes. 'Tell Repple to stop the mechanism. Stop the main wheel. Stop it now!'

There was excitement and anticipation in her steps as she hurtled down the stairs full pelt. Not too late then, not yet. She had to get to Repple. Save Freddie, and the world. Simple.

The Doctor was now struggling to escape from Wyse, not to hold on to him. With a shout of anger and determination, he wrenched himself free, rolled over, leaped to his feet. He spared Melissa a glance. She was still working at the mechanism attached to the hammer, scrabbling at it with her long fingers in the split second the hammer was still before crashing into the side of the bell as it struck the hour. Hoping to disable Wyse's device so that if they survived this time it didn't just start again when the clock next struck.

Maybe she was doing it because there was nothing else she could do. Or maybe she was confident that the Doctor could still save them. That possibility of her returned trust galvanised him, and with a final angry kick at Wyse the Doctor raced for the stairs.

Rose clattered past the clock room. 'I'm coming, Freddie,' she shouted, as she kept going, down to the prisoner's room and the main mechanism.

The huge cogwheel was already beginning to turn. Repple and the Mechanical had torn apart a separate piece of the mechanism and had a metal bar thrust in between the cog's teeth. But even as Rose watched, the bar snapped, the broken end disappearing behind the cog as if being eaten by some industrial monster.

'You have to stop it!' she shouted.

Behind her, another figure ran into the room. The Doctor. 'Oh, about time!' Rose said. Clutching the sonic screwdriver tightly like a talisman, she turned to run back out, to go to Freddie, her heart pounding.

But Wyse was running down the stairs. His eyes burned with anger. Instinctively, Rose thrust the sonic screwdriver at him, hoping to drive him backwards, out of her way. Instead, he held his ground. He grabbed the sonic screwdriver, tore it from her hand and threw it across the room.

It clattered along the floor, rolling and bouncing – into the heart of the mechanism. Rose ran back, her legs about to give way, feeling sick as she saw it – the sonic screwdriver, resting on a ledge that was one of the teeth of the huge cogwheel. Rising slowly but inexorably towards the teeth of a small wheel. Smaller, but still capable of crushing the screwdriver to pieces.

Without thought, Rose hurled herself after it. She landed on a rotating platform in the middle of the machinery. Lying on her stomach, being slowly swung towards the teeth of the cog, reaching out for the sonic screwdriver, hoping to pluck it from the cogwheel before it was crushed.

Knowing she would be too late.

Her arm caught on the ragged edge of the cog, her hand closing on the sonic screwdriver but unable to pull back. Wrenched painfully upwards, towards the descending metal that would crush her hand and wrist.

And the platform turned, bringing her under the teeth of the cog on the other side. Teeth about to bite through her as the final sequence clicked into motion and the last chimes of Big Ben faded into the night.

EIGHTEEN

The Mechanical raised its arm. A blade sliced through the air, but missed Wyse as he dived back up the stairs outside the room. The Mechanical reached the door, and turned to fire again. But there was a dull click from its arm as the spring activated and found no blades left.

Wyse leaped to his feet. The Mechanical was on the stairs now, cutting off Wyse's escape to his ship and forcing him upwards again – back towards the top of the tower.

'Wait,' the Doctor shouted to the Mechanical. 'Help me get Rose! Find something to jam the wheel.'

Repple was standing beside the machinery. He watched the cogwheel click upwards, the teeth meshing together, Rose being dragged into the closing mouth of iron. 'Too late, Doctor.'

He stepped forward as the gap began to close round Rose's trapped hand and the sonic screwdriver. He leaned as far as he could into the mechanism. In a single fluid motion, Repple pushed his hand and arm between the biting teeth, in the slot above where Rose's hand was trapped.

The machinery groaned and shuddered. Repple screamed. Rose managed to get to her feet as the platform slowed and stopped. It clicked forward slightly, making her stagger. But her hand was free, and she had the sonic screwdriver.

Reaching in past Repple, the Doctor grabbed Rose round the waist and heaved her out. He looked at Repple, nodded in thanks, then ran after Wyse. 'Help him,' he said to the waiting Mechanical as he passed. 'Stop the wheel from turning.'

Rose was pale and weak. 'Thank you,' she managed to say to Repple.

'Help Freddie,' Repple gasped in reply. The wheel was struggling to turn. Repple was dragged further into the mechanism as the teeth bit deeper into his arm. 'He shouldn't be alone.'

She hesitated a moment, watching as Repple was pulled another step into the machinery. Wondering why there was no blood, why instead of the crunch of bone she could hear the tearing of metal. Then the Mechanical gently moved her aside. The spell broken, she turned and ran.

Repple looked at the Mechanical. 'Do it,' he said, and closed his eyes against the pain.

The Mechanical stepped forward. It gripped Repple's shoulder firmly with one gauntlet, and the top of his trapped arm with the other.

Rose stood in the doorway of the room above, sonic screwdriver clutched so hard in her hand that it hurt. She stared dumbly at the trail of blood across the floor, from the corner out through the doorway and on to the stairs. The clock ticked away the seconds she stood there. She knew he could not have moved on his own.

But the room was empty. Freddie was gone.

The Doctor exploded into the belfry. He threw himself under the bells, rolling across the wooden platform.

'Over here.' The voice was calm. Melissa was standing beside Big Ben. She was holding the remains of the device Wyse had attached to the hammer. She was not looking at the Doctor, but staring at the back wall of the tower, at the shadows between one of the arched openings.

Where, at the edge of the tower, stood Wyse. He had retrieved the gun. He was holding it in front of the frightened face of Freddie. The boy could hardly stand. The Doctor saw the tourniquet round his upper thigh, the blood ebbing slowly from his scratched leg. Drip, drip, drip. Second by second. Like the tick of a clock. He remembered Rose's face close to his, her urgency. He felt suddenly dead inside.

'You've lost, Wyse,' the Doctor said. He hoped the tremors he felt were not echoed in his voice.

'I don't think so, old chap.' Wyse seemed to have reverted to his previous gentlemanly manner. 'Those dolts downstairs won't be able to stop the mechanism. Oh, they might slow it down. Give it something to chew on, as it were. But I do fancy I can hear it starting up again, don't you?'

The Doctor could. There was a whine of power, of wheels and gears grinding into motion, echoing up from the ventilation shaft. Had Melissa disarmed it? Would that be enough if she had? 'Let the boy go,' he said.

'Oh no. I need this little chappie to get me out of here. Past your mechanical friend on the stairs.'

'And if we don't let you leave?' Melissa asked.

Wyse shook his head in apparent disappointment. 'You really don't have any imagination at all, do you?' he said sadly. His face twisted abruptly into a savage mask, and he dragged Freddie back, to the very edge of the clock tower, leaning him over. The boy's eyes were wide with fear, his face pale as paper.

'I'd rather not waste any more bullets,' Wyse said. 'After all, I might need them for you.' He pulled Freddie back to safety, though still perilously close to the edge. 'Can you hear it?' he whispered. 'The wheels are turning once more. The process begins.'

The massive cogwheel lurched round again. The remains of Repple's arm – outwardly human, still in the sleeve of his jacket, but spilling brass screws and flywheels – crunched under the weight. Another lurch, and the machinery whirred into more healthy life.

'It's starting again,' Repple said. 'We need something more substantial.' He stepped towards the wheel, closing his eyes and stretching out his remaining arm.

A hand closed heavily on his good shoulder, turning him round. Repple opened his eyes and saw the blank gunmetal face of the Mechanical close to his own. Then the world seemed to turn upside down as he was hurled across the room, away from the machinery.

The Mechanical watched Repple slam into the wall and slide to the floor. It waited just long enough to see that he was not damaged, but stunned enough not to interfere. Then it turned back to the mass of machinery. It stepped forward and reached inside the wheels and gears as they began to turn freely. Its voice was a mechanical rasp, barely audible above the straining mechanism.

'Even machines...' it said.

Then the squealing sound of tearing metal, of straining gears, of machinery slamming to a halt and wrenching itself apart drowned out the rest of its words. If they ever came.

The cog rocked slightly, straining to move. Then with a final explosion of breaking iron, its huge spindle snapped and the wheel toppled sideways. It crashed down towards Repple, the top of it smacking into the wall above him. Metal teeth biting into the stonework.

Silence.

Except for a sound like the ticking of a clock.

There was a smell of burning. In the seconds of silence following the wrenching, tearing sound from below, Wyse had stood open-mouthed and astonished. Now he was livid. He aimed the gun straight at the Doctor.

'No!' Rose ran into the belfry and leaped across the bridge over the platform.

Wyse turned, and fired at her in one movement. But Freddie shoved his arm upwards and the shot missed. The bullet clanged into the inside of one of the quarter bells, rattling and ricocheting. The noise was deafening. Rose clapped her hands over her ears.

Startled and deafened, Wyse let go of Freddie. But instead of trying to escape, the boy grabbed hold of Wyse – pushing him back towards the edge of the tower.

'Freddie!' the Doctor shouted as the sound died away.

'I'm dead anyway,' Freddie said, his voice strained, weak, but determined. Another step towards the edge.

'No, Freddie!' Rose screamed at him. She ran to grab him, to pull him back.

Wyse teetered on the very edge of the tower, then managed to push Freddie roughly away. Rose caught the boy as he staggered and fell. She fell with him.

'You've lost, Wyse,' the Doctor said.

'It's finished,' Melissa agreed. 'Too many people have died for you, even here on Earth.'

But Wyse seemed to have recovered his composure. 'It was you who killed them.'

'An accident,' she snapped back. 'I thought it was worth it. But I was wrong. You're not worth anyone's life. This is the end.'

'For now, perhaps,' Wyse conceded. He had the gun aimed at Rose as she nursed Freddie on the floor in front of him. 'But I can still walk out of here.'

Rose barely heard him. She was holding the sonic screwdriver over Freddie's wounded leg. 'What do I do?' she shouted. The boy's eyes were closed. 'Doctor, what do I do?'

'You come with me,' Wyse told her. 'A far more robust and useful hostage, don't you think, Doctor?' He gave a short laugh. 'I take your queen. Checkmate.'

The Doctor did not answer. He was looking down at the floor, as if depressed, as if ready to accept the inevitable. But Rose could see what he was looking at. She realised what he was thinking, what he was planning to do. And ducked.

It had limped slowly and silently across the platform under the bells, slipping between the Doctor's feet. Now the cat was staring at Wyse, its green eyes gleaming. The Doctor's kick propelled it through the air, straight at Wyse. Straight at the man's head – claws out, hissing with anger.

Wyse gave a startled cry. He took a step backwards and threw up his arms to protect himself as the cat's eyes glowed weakly. The claws raked down his hand and the gun fell forgotten at his feet.

The cat snarled – mouth open wide, sharp teeth bared. It clawed and tore at Wyse, latching on to his collar and ripping at his face. He had the cat round the neck, dragging it clear, trying to avoid the flailing paws.

But too late. Already off balance, the cat's renewed attack drove him back, to the edge of the tower. He was caught for the briefest instant, one tick of the clock, on the brink. Then he was toppling backwards, screaming, falling. The cat's face was close to his own. The air rushing past them, tearing the breath from him.

The cat's eyes fixed on Wyse's terrified realisation as he fell through the fog. Its voice was a metallic scrape, like the protesting gears of a broken mechanism.

'Got you!' the cat said.

NINETEEN

Melissa was wearing her happy face when she said good-bye. Presumably she thought it was appropriate. Rose didn't.

'We remained undetected and I have completed my mission,' she explained simply.

'Despite losing your crew,' Repple pointed out.

She shrugged. 'They were just Mechanicals.' But there was a hint of regret in her voice. Repple did not reply.

'Lucky the cat was there,' Rose said.

'It *was* a black cat,' the Doctor pointed out. 'Though I did have a deal to offer Wyse if all else failed.'

'You knew how to power up his ship?' Melissa asked in surprise.

The Doctor shook his head. 'I was going to give him yours.'

'I shall miss this strange planet with its ugly-looking people,' Melissa confessed as she and the Doctor shook hands on the Embankment.

'They won't all miss you.'

She inclined her head, perhaps in sorrow. 'Vassily is dead,' she said quietly, 'and I have destroyed his body. I have succeeded, but it was not worth the cost.' Rose and Repple watched from the other side of the road.

The three of them stood together a few minutes later, watching as the surface of the Thames seemed to heave upwards. The slick, dark shape of Melissa's ship detached itself from the water and lifted soundlessly into the night sky. It paused over their heads, as if bidding farewell, then with a streak of impossibly bright light it was gone.

'One more job to do,' the Doctor said. They walked to Sir George's house in silence.

Repple waited for them outside. The Doctor let Rose do the talking. Sir George sat silently listening, his hands clasped tightly in his lap and his face pale as death.

'He was a hero,' Rose said. 'He really was. He saved us all, several times. He was so…' She couldn't think of the words and looked away.

Sir George leaned forward and put his hand over Rose's. 'Yes, he was. Such enthusiasm, such love of life. Such a willingness to help. Always wanting to help – in the house, the garden, the kitchen.' He smiled sadly. 'Drives his mother potty, you know. No wonder she worries about him so.'

'She will be all right?' Rose asked quietly.

Sir George nodded. 'I'm sure she will. She's very strong, you know. But she's been through a lot in her life. Like Freddie.'

'I'm sorry,' the Doctor said quietly. It was the first time he had spoken since they arrived.

'That's all right, Doctor,' Sir George said. 'We'll be fine now. And you never know...' He stood up and shook the Doctor's hand. 'It might have shocked some sense into the boy.' He smiled weakly. The smile turned to a look of surprise as Rose hugged him tight. 'I say, steady on.'

There were tears on her cheeks when she stepped away. 'Give Freddie our love, won't you. And Anna. He may not remember that we said goodbye.'

'Indeed I will.' Sir George glanced upwards as he spoke.

And in the room above, a mother sat on her son's bed, holding his pale, cold hand. She cried soundless tears. Tears of relief and joy as she felt every weak rhythm of his pulse. Tears that became sobs as he opened his eyes, and managed to smile.

Then his eyes closed again and he slept on peacefully – dreaming of clocks and cats and cogwheels. And of how he had been a hero.

The reassuring blue shape of the TARDIS was standing at the back of Melissa's house. Just as she had promised.

'I'm surprised you trusted her,' Rose said.

The Doctor clicked his tongue. 'You've no faith.' He turned to Repple. 'Goodbye, then.'

Repple reached out to shake first the Doctor's hand, then Rose's.

'I like the new arm,' she said. 'And thanks. You know.' She held on to his hand for a moment. It was like the gauntlet of a medieval armoured knight. The fingers were jointed metal, the hand was stiff and cold. His arm was plain gunmetal, attached – expertly, the Doctor claimed proudly – to the shoulder.

Except that Rose couldn't see the arm, because it was hidden beneath Repple's new coat. A battered brown leather jacket.

'It's no good to me,' the Doctor had sighed. 'Stitching's coming apart.'

When she let go, Repple lifted up his hand in front of his face, inspecting it. Behind his expressionless face Rose knew was a mass of cogs and gears and sprockets. It was hard to believe. He seemed so ordinary. So human.

'I don't think the previous owner will be needing the arm back,' the Doctor reassured him. 'Sorry it's not more in keeping.'

'Thank you, Doctor.' He flexed his fingers, then let the arm drop to his side. 'It reminds me of who I really am.'

'The AI's gone,' the Doctor said. 'Burned out and disintegrated. So there's nothing to stop you leaving, assuming there ever really was. We can give you a lift, if you want,' he offered.

'Where to? This is the only home I have.'

The Doctor nodded. 'See you then.'

'You'll do all right,' Rose said. 'Hey, if you're still around in eighty years or so, come and visit me.'

'Thank you. Perhaps I will.' He stepped back, and surprised Rose by snapping a salute.

'Don't get lonely,' she said.

The Doctor opened the door of the TARDIS, and she followed him inside.

The blue box faded from reality with a grating, rasping sound. For a moment the empty outline of the TARDIS was stamped in the gathering fog.

Repple stood watching the shape blur and fade as the mist drifted across. Then, with a barely perceptible whirr of internal gears, he turned and walked back to the front of the house.

He paused in the glow of a street light, listening to the breeze ruffle the autumn leaves and the distant chimes of Big Ben. He imagined he could feel that breeze on his face, that he could smell the stink of the river. And he tried to ignore the rhythmic ticking that kept him constant company. He waited for the black cat that wandered lazily down the road to catch him up. It regarded him curiously through deep, emerald eyes.

The first traces of dawn were scattered across the skyline, silhouetting the Palace of Westminster, as the two of them started their journey.

Acknowledgements

I am indebted to a number of people who have helped with this novel, and thank them all.

In particular, I should mention everyone who is involved in the production of the new series of *Doctor Who*, but especially Russell T Davies – for his help, advice, encouragement and contagious enthusiasm – and script editors Helen Raynor and Elwen Rowlands, who have kept me honest and provided invaluable insight into the characters of the Doctor and Rose.

My editor, Steve Cole, has continued to work wonders, making me look good in print and providing sympathy, friendship, and beer. Working with him and with Jac Rayner on these novels has been a labour of love in the best sense.

And finally, I must thank my MP, James Plaskitt, for arranging a guided tour of the clock tower at the Palace of Westminster. Inside it is pretty much as I describe it, though I have made some small changes for dramatic reasons – there is, for example (and so far as I could tell), no infernal alien device ready to fry the Earth's atmosphere.

About the author

Justin Richards is the Creative Director for the BBC Books *Doctor Who* series, and has written a fair few of them himself. As well as writing for stage, screen and audio, he is the author of *The Invisible Detective* novels for children. His novel for older children, *The Death Collector*, will be published in 2006.

Justin lives in Warwick, with a lovely view of the famous castle but no cat. Being married with two children, his life is never dull and never runs like clockwork.